FORGING THE GUILD

The Protector Guild Book 2

GRAY HOLBORN

Copyright © 2021 by Gray Holborn

All rights reserved.

No part of this book may be reproduced in any form or by any electronic or mechanical means, including information storage and retrieval systems, without written permission from the author, except for the use of brief quotations in a book review.

ISBN: 9798880159840

Edits: CopybyKath

Design: DamoroDesigns

I
DECLAN

The vampire's head went rolling down the hall like a child's toy. I did my best to ignore the gross squelching sounds echoing around us—an almost impossible feat. With some careful footwork, I successfully avoided stepping into any of the puddles of blood. I wasn't exactly squeamish, but if I could avoid bathing in the gore, I did. Atlas covered my six, but even with the absurd circumstances, I couldn't keep the grin from my face.

Six. The two of us had taken down a group of six vampires and werewolves, without suffering more than a few superficial scrapes and bruises. And the deeper ones would be completely healed up by morning. The surprise ambush worked like a perfectly-choreographed execution. We had two of them impaled through the heart before they even realized we were there. Even though Atlas was just as silent and hyper vigilant as always, I knew him well enough to know that he was equally smug. That sort of ratio was unheard of.

And I couldn't lie, I was pretty pleased with myself. Plus, it felt great to get to end a few of those fuckers before they had the chance to take down any more humans. I pulled my hair up into a high ponytail, cringing as I wiped a wet streak of blood off my neck. A gross ligament chunk or something flew from my hand to the floor, but I forced myself not to think about it. Hunting supernatural creatures from the hell realm wasn't exactly glamorous work.

The warehouse was a dark labyrinth, with winding halls and doors leading to different paths. Clearing this place was like a choose-your-own-adventure novel. Our guards were up, but the place was so quiet that I doubted there were any other monsters lying in wait. Beasts like these rarely opted for subtlety. A soft glow from down the hall offered enough light to see each step we took. But just in case there were more creatures hanging around, we slowed our pace, moving as silently as possible.

Truthfully, we were extremely lucky with this win. Our intel suggested there was only a slight possibility that there were any wolves here at all—the fact that we found vamps working with them as well was going to blow the roof off our theories back home. Atlas was our team leader and if he'd been following protocol, we'd have reported the information in before taking the group down. But our team had a few grudges where this pack of wolves was concerned, and way too much ego to wait.

We were lucky this time, and hopefully with the win, we wouldn't get much more than a light slap on the wrist for breaking the rules.

As soon as that thought crossed my mind, I pushed open the door and wished with all of my being that I could take everything back. That we had called in our findings and waited for instruction before entering the warehouse.

The room was bathed in a swathe of warm light from a large chandelier and dozens of candles. A giant, opulent table stood in the middle of the room, covered with plates of delicious-looking food. Some of the cutlery and platters were littered along the floor, but so still and disregarded that it almost seemed intentional, like a surreal post-party painting. That was the least remarkable sight though, as I watched large puddles of blood sink into the dark carpet.

As soon as I saw him, I choked on a cry and forced myself to swallow back the tears budding along my lash line. Wade, Atlas's little brother, was lying on the ground, surrounded by the carcasses of what looked like three werewolves and a vampire. While we'd been busy dealing with the beasts in the lobby and exploring the north end of the building as discreetly as possible, Wade had been here, handling these assholes on his own.

As if on autopilot, my eyes scanned the room again. Where the hell was Eli? Why did we think it was a reasonable idea to split up? We shouldn't have entered the building without calling it in. Eli was right. Wade was right. God-fucking-damnit. Atlas and I had let our petty attempts at revenge cloud our judgment. Wade, if he—if this was on us—

It wasn't the sort of thing we could come back from, least of all Atlas.

Atlas reached me in the short second it took me to take everything in; the only tell that he processed the scene came from a low, heartbreakingly pain-filled inhale. If Wade was dead, Atlas would never forgive himself. And then we would have as good as lost two members of our team tonight. All because of our fucking hubris.

Leaving Atlas, I ran to Wade and crouched down before pressing my fingers into his pulse point. I couldn't hear anything but a low whistle, as the blood rushed to my head; couldn't feel anything except for a frantic pounding in my chest. There was so much blood, too much blood. My hands were shaking so badly that it took me several seconds to discern whether or not his heart was still beating.

"He's alive," I said, the words tumbling out on a harsh breath. I half believed it myself. Alive. His pulse was breathy, far too weak. But if we got him on the plane fast enough, he might stand a chance. It was all we had.

When I didn't hear Atlas's harsh steps behind me any longer, I turned around, afraid more creatures were gearing up for a second attack. What I saw nearly broke me. Atlas was huddled back by the door, staring at his brother with a vacant look in his deep brown eyes. It was almost like he couldn't convince his legs to step further into the room. His usually stylishly messy hair was plastered in soft waves against his forehead from a layer of sweat. Even with his face slightly shadowed, I could tell that his usually tanned skin had lost most of its color.

"Atlas, did you hear me?" I whisper-yelled as I fished through my clothes for my phone. I dialed Eli's number, desperate for him to pick up. If he was as bad off as Wade was, we didn't stand a chance of getting them both back in time. I glanced around the room again, making sure that Eli's body wasn't hidden by one of the corpses.

Atlas shook his head and steadied his eyes on me, staring as my words slowly filtered through his mind. I could see the tearless sob pulse through his body.

"Where the hell are you guys?" Eli's deep voice whispered into the phone. I let out a desperate breath. He was alive—okay. Or at least okay enough to answer the phone call with that annoying, bored sarcasm of his. "I can't find Wade anywhere and I don't have visuals on any baddies."

Quickly, I filled him in, trying to provide directions to our location with the brief knowledge I had of the building's layout. Rather than risk him running into any remaining rogues, I told him to meet us back at the plane.

"He's alive," I said again, loud enough for Atlas to hear. I wanted so badly to provide a soft comfort, to snap him out of it, without giving him too much hope. Hope could be a dangerous promise sometimes. "I don't know how bad it is. He's beaten up. Badly. But he's alive. We need to get him out of here. Now."

All at once, my words breathed movement into Atlas's limbs and he pushed through the room, narrowly avoiding tripping on a dead wolf. He blinked twice, staring at the angles of the wolf's body.

In death it looked like a grotesque stuffed animal, and I swallowed back bile, my brain briefly considering whether this was one of the wolves who had killed Sarah, who had fractured our lives once already. Who had destroyed Atlas's. And now, again, here we were. It was like we were living on this unforgiving, painful loop. It was a carousel ride I wanted off of immediately.

When he reached me, his knees buckled. As if he wouldn't let himself hope, wouldn't let himself believe me, he pressed his fingers against Wade's pulse, unwilling to let himself breathe until he felt a steady hum.

"Help me get him out of here, Atlas," I said again, my words low but firm. "We need to get back to The Guild. He looks bad." I could carry him on my own, if I had to, but we'd go faster if I had help. Atlas was the strongest on the team.

I glanced briefly at the wounds seeping with blood. It was impossible to tell how bad they were, and all I could smell was death. I tensed my hands into fists, hoping that the odor was from the wolves and vampire and not this kid who had been like a little brother to me for most of my life. With a nod, he picked Wade up, sharing the weight with me. We made our way swiftly out of the warehouse and back to the plane. My mind fluttered briefly over the fact that we didn't meet any other creatures on our way out. Why had they just left him there like that—still breathing and clinging to life? Any other mission, this would have set off warnings, but I didn't have time to focus on protector mode right now.

"Jesus," Eli said, as he caught up to us. His face was pale and the usual mirth that covered his features was gone. It was like looking at the ghost of Eli Bentley. "Is he—Jesus, please tell me he's alive?"

We climbed into the plane and took off as soon as the door closed. "For now."

As soon as the plane safely left the ground, I hooked Wade up to an IV, setting up a shoddy transfusion. It was protocol to keep blood on hand in the back refrigerator for moments like this. Unfortunately, in our line of work, this sort of thing happened all too frequently. Protectors, especially those of us who focused on field work, had a short shelf life. While we were significantly stronger than humans, our senses and strength didn't come nearly close enough to being on level with the monsters we hunted. That's why protectors were put into field teams—strength in numbers helped even the playing field a bit.

Eli helped get him hooked up, his fingers pressed gently against Wade's pulse as he waited for signs of improvement. I could tell by his steady focus that Eli's usual flight anxiety was completely eclipsed by fear for his teammate instead. I let Eli take the reins since he was the best at field medicine in our group. It was a surprising skill of his. Eli didn't take his work or The Guild nearly as seriously as the rest of us. But when it came down to it, he could cast his cynicism aside and do what was necessary. Hell, if he actually put more effort in, he could probably give even Atlas a run for his money.

After we did everything we could for him with the supplies from the plane, we sat back down, monitoring him closely for any change. Protectors healed extremely quickly, especially compared to humans, but I had a feeling we wouldn't see much improvement from Wade before we got back.

My shirt was soaked through with his blood, the strong metallic smell making it impossible for me to let my mind wander too far from him or the visuals of that room—the strange opulence of a feast mixed with the gore of a horror film.

I turned to Atlas, frowning at the look on his face. I could read his thoughts as if they were my own. If Wade didn't make it, he would be done with The Guild, with us. He was done losing everyone he was meant to protect. Every protector had their hard limit—the point of no return that broke them—and Wade's life would be his.

2
MAX

"Seriously girl, you freaked me out," Izzy said, her candy-apple red lips twisting into a lopsided grin. Her short dark hair bobbed slightly as she flung a slice of pizza around with each word. Izzy was one of those people who always seemed so completely full of life; her eyes always dancing with mirth, her light brown skin constantly glowing with warmth. "I mean, I have these grand plans to turn you into my best friend, and then you immediately go and almost die on me. Not cool, my dude, not cool. From now on, you travel with a buddy at all times."

About a week ago, I was attacked by a vampire outside of the local Guild-owned bar. And she was right, I did almost die, but here I was. Glamorous? No. But it sure as hell was one way to create a splash in this school.

Ro chuckled, his left dimple carving into his cheek. He had taken a liking to Izzy during my days of rest. Something about her constantly pestering him for updates about me had him convinced she was good people. He'd also collected the field team of his new crush, Arnell, as dinner company, though I was surprised to find that he was all but ignoring Arnell tonight. Every so often, I'd see them catch each other's eye, but Ro

7

would break contact almost immediately, quick to join a conversation with almost anyone else at the table.

"Won't happen again," I promised, shaking off my concern over Ro. I'd find out what happened between them eventually. Ro was the sort of guy who would open up, but only on his own terms. As his sister, I found the waiting period to often be infuriating, but I'd learned well enough to leave him to his process.

Izzy winked, her gray eyes dancing with mirth. "Somehow I doubt that, Max. You're the type to draw trouble in at all opportunities. I can tell. Next time, just make sure I'm there to join in."

Arnell awkwardness aside, it was strange to see how well Ro had begun to fit in with everyone while I was in the infirmary and under house arrest. And even more strange to feel like I'd missed out on a lifetime of events when I'd only been on 'bed rest' for a few days. I couldn't complain though, falling into a group now that I was back was really nice. I'd been getting so many suspicious looks since I returned and had been the center of so many rumors, that it was a relief to have a group of friends I could surround myself with.

And weirdly, I felt great. Vampire bites almost always either killed or permanently damaged protectors. But the bite on my neck had disappeared in less than a day. It was nothing short of a miracle.

Ro and I arrived at The Guild just a short week or so ago, and I was surprised to find that I felt so at home here, so attached to people already. I barely knew Izzy, but I could already tell that she was one of those friends who would be an important part of my life. And while I didn't know all of the members of Team Ten super well, I liked them a lot, liked being absorbed into their group and odd little chosen family.

Ro and I were adopted by our grumpy guardian, Cyrus. Before moving to The Guild, I'd spent my entire life living deep in the woods, with almost no opportunities for socializing or learning about the world of protectors.

Protectors were descendants of angels and our whole purpose in life was to protect humanity from vamps, wolves, and various demons that escaped from the hell realm. We were also charged with keeping the supernatural world a secret, which meant that Cyrus avoided socializing with humans like the plague. Since we didn't grow up around a protector compound, that meant Ro and I only really had each other for company. Until now.

Shaking my head, I turned back towards Arnell and Sharla. I didn't know either of them particularly well, but they both had something about them that drew me in. They both fought like badasses, but there was a softness to their personalities that seemed quite rare for protectors to hold onto. This lifestyle had a tendency to harden people at young ages. But like Izzy, Arnell and Sharla just radiated warmth.

"How often does your team go out on missions?" I'd been frustrated by Atlas's outright rejection of me, but I liked all the members of Ten—even Jer, who had toned down the overt flirtation a bit. Maybe they'd let Ro and I shadow them some time soon.

I had learned during my lessons that at nineteen years of age, The Guild let protectors-in-training observe missions from safe distances, and occasionally even join teams as graduates. Kind of like job shadowing, only significantly more dangerous. My birthday was still a little over a month away, but I was itching to watch a real mission. Especially after getting cornered by a vamp—I wanted to fast forward and get to butt kicking.

"Generally, we get called out every two weeks or so." Jer was the one who answered, his unusual reddish black hair reflecting the cafeteria's light. His warm, honey-colored eyes met mine and I forced down the blush threatening to take over. He had a way of studying me closely, a feeling that left me jittery with nerves more often than not.

I didn't know him well enough to know if those nerves were the start of a blossoming crush or not. My experience in that department was seriously lacking.

"But," Sharla continued, picking up where he left off, "it really depends on whatever situation we're responding to. Since there's been such an increase in supe activity lately, we've been getting called in more frequently. All teams have."

I suppressed a shiver at the reminder. During my time at The Guild, I had learned that there had been an increase in vamp and wolf attacks in recent years—but that the number and strength of attacks had been increasing at an unprecedented rate this year especially. In fact, the monsters were even starting to boldly infiltrate protector boundaries, something they'd never done before. It was why my attack had come as such a surprise. Rumors and theories had been spreading through campus like wildfire, and unfortunately, I was at the center of all of that attention. But the layer of fear coating The Guild was impossible to ignore. There was talk that they were going to institute a new rule that wouldn't allow students to leave campus without having a member of an official team present, just in case.

Arnell nodded, tossing his leftover pizza crust back on his plate. "Yeah, we are one of the younger teams, so they tend to throw us softballs." He got up, collecting everyone's empty trays before leaving us to drop them all off. He cast Ro a quick, loaded glance, his lips turning down in a slight frown. Ro's bright blue eyes immediately dipped to his lap as he started fidgeting with the hem of his shirt.

Jer laughed quietly, shaking his hair out of his eyes. "Plus, one of the younger recruits swears she saw a werewolf in the woods, so now security is tightening even more. I'm sure that means we'll have to do extra rounds and whatnot until anxieties die down a bit."

"A werewolf? On campus?" Ro's brows angled down, a fierceness emanating from his guarded expression. "Seriously?"

"She probably just had too much to drink and confused a regular wolf with a supernatural one. No one else has seen one. Trust me, these sorts of false alarms get called all the time—half of our missions are based on faulty leads and misinformation."

Jer wiped some crumbs on his pant legs, pushing himself back slightly from the table.

"Don't worry, Max," Sharla added, swiping on some clear lip gloss. Between her deep skin tone and blue eyes, the girl was stunning enough to grace magazine covers. "Once Headmistress Alleva is back, I think you'll be allowed to observe or even participate in one of our missions, if you'd like." Her fingers squeezed my forearm lightly. "I mean, you've already survived a vamp attack solo, which is more than anyone here has done. I'm sure they're dying to get you paired up with a team as soon as possible. I wouldn't be surprised if they eventually push you towards one of the top teams."

Outside of my family, Izzy, and Atlas's Team Six, no one knew that I didn't exactly survive the vamp attack off just my own merits. I was rescued last minute by a giant hellhound named Ralph. And I'd learned pretty quickly that hellhounds weren't the norm for our world. As far as anyone knew, nobody had encountered one before and survived.

So now, because of me, Ralph was currently housed in a creepy dungeon, while Guild researchers ran tests, trying to determine if he was dangerous or not. Rather than incite panic on campus, I was sworn to secrecy about his existence. I didn't know enough people to struggle too much with the secret-keeping part. But I was having a seriously rough time pretending to be okay with how The Guild treated the hero of my story.

I broke eye contact with Sharla, uncomfortable that I had to lie to my new friends about Ralph. And I was equally uncomfortable with taking credit for a win I hadn't earned on my own. Surviving a vamp attack solo was no small feat. The entire campus was starstruck by Cyrus because he managed to survive fighting off two by himself. The guy was apparently a legend.

Which was a weird thing to learn—that the grumpy guy who raised me was basically a celebrity in our world. It made his decision to live in the middle of the woods, away from his responsibilities, an odd choice.

"Besides," Sharla added, "with heightened vamp and werewolf incidents lately, I think Alleva's in a rush to get new recruits out into the field."

Atlas's half-brother Wade had mentioned something similar to me during our last tutoring session.

"Cyrus and Seamus approved Ro to observe our mission tonight, so I'm sure you'll be next—we've all seen you fight. And you'll be nineteen soon, right?" Jer asked, his face lighting up with a flirtatious grin.

"Shit," Ro muttered. He ducked his head slightly, scratching the back of his neck. He caught my eye briefly before looking away again and fiddling with his nails. They were all bitten low, a nervous habit of his. He'd been trying to break it for as long as I could remember. "I was going to tell you," he cleared his throat, "eventually."

"What?" I stood, staring down at him. "You're going on a mission?" It was weird to see different rules apply to Ro. Sure he was a year older than I was, but I'd been so used to us being trained in everything together. Cy always made us seem equal in his eyes, and we'd always reached milestones in our training together. I wasn't accustomed to the rush of jealousy that flooded my stomach. As soon as I saw the side of his lips pull down though, I swallowed it back. I refused to be jealous, not of Ro. "That's amazing. You'll have to tell me everything when you get back."

I knew that true mirth and excitement were missing from my voice, but I couldn't be expected to be *that* big of a person. I would definitely be talking to Cy later, convincing him to let me observe as soon as possible.

Part of me was just frustrated that Ro was fitting in with a new team—and doing so without me being a part of that puzzle too. But it wasn't Ro's fault that I wasn't included.

Before Atlas and the rest of his team left, he'd made it abundantly clear that as far as he was concerned, I would never belong with their group. So between that flat-out rejection, and now Ro's new place with a team, I was feeling left behind and unsettled. I'd missed out on way too much recovering from the vamp attack.

※

AFTER TWENTY-FOUR HOURS OF NONSTOP TRAINING AND reading, I was getting restless. Atlas and the rest of his team still weren't back and Cyrus changed the subject every time I brought up Ralph or asked to go see him. Ro's mission wasn't nearly as exciting as either of us thought it would be—he didn't run into a single other realm beast and instead spent most of his evening camped out on a concrete building, just to return back to Headquarters early in the morning. Still, while it sucked that he was bored and disappointed, I was beyond relieved when he showed up back home in one piece.

They'd been given false information about some werewolf activity. They didn't even run into a single werewolf, let alone a pack. So basically we'd seen more monster activity in our tiny town before even joining The Guild.

The only cool thing Ro learned on the trip was that The Guild owned several small planes that teams got to take out if they were heading more than two hundred miles away from the base. It wasn't particularly fancy, but neither of us had been on a plane before, so it was still exciting to live vicariously through his experience. My fingers were crossed that my first mission would be a decent way away.

And somewhere warm.

Or anywhere, really. I'd been to exactly two places: our old cabin and The Guild. I was ready to start collecting some stamps in my passport.

Jer was the primary person in charge of my training and Arnell and Sharla had taken over the private lessons that Wade was supposed to be leading. After taking down Jer during more than half of our spars, I was almost missing having Atlas and Eli around. Almost.

Jer was a lot nicer and much more receptive to my friendship than the members of Six had been. And he didn't cause my temper to rise nearly as often as the others did.

Izzy, Ro, and I were eating dinner with Ten, laughing about that afternoon's training match, in which Izzy had taken down Jer, who was still overcoming his exhaustion from the night before, when Cyrus abruptly rose from his seat across the cafeteria. Something about his rigid posture instantly caught my eye, and I knew without the shadow of a doubt that the temporary peace over the last few days was about to shatter.

He quietly looked around the room, his long black hair swinging around him. His face looked drawn and paler than usual. In a quick flurry, he left through the wide front doors, texting furiously on his phone; which was unusual because I think he had used a phone maybe twice in all the time that I knew him.

I met Ro's eyes immediately and could tell that he'd been tracking Cy too. We both stood up at the same time, without a single word needed, before discarding our trays and swiftly leaving the cafeteria. For once, our stack of pizza slices lost all appeal. Which was something that I didn't think was even possible under most circumstances. Apparently tracking Cyrus down and seeing what was going on was the best way to limit my caloric intake. At least temporarily.

"Oh no you don't, I'm not getting left behind. I'm going too," Izzy said, huffing out a breath as she caught up with us. Shaking her head, she glanced between the two of us and let out a musical chuckle, small laugh lines creasing at her eyes. "Wow, you totally forgot I was even sitting with you, didn't you? Well, whatever the rush is, I'm in. You get into all sorts of trouble without me. So let's go stalk your prey together." With a wink, turn, and a skip, she led the way out into the night. Ro glanced at me and shrugged before following her.

"Any idea what this is about?" she whispered, after we followed Cyrus past most of the buildings we were familiar with.

The night was dark, a soft glow from the moon lighting our path as he wove around trees and old vine-addled buildings. We were far away from where most of our classes were housed, so I had a feeling we were winding our way through a lot of private residences for transient Guild members.

Cy was about fifty feet ahead of us when he whipped his head back, his intelligent eyes combing through the landscape. We pushed forward a few paces before landing behind a tree just as Cy's gaze reached where we'd been standing a moment before. It wasn't the most stealthy move I'd ever done, but if Cyrus knew he was being followed, he didn't let on.

"Nope," I answered, my whisper probably a few notches too loud. "But Cyrus looked worried, and he's been keeping things quiet since we got here, so I'm not going inside until I have some answers."

In my short time at Headquarters, I felt like the Cy I knew and loved was slowly slipping away from my reach. He'd kept so many secrets and been so busy with mystery missions with field teams that I hardly even saw him anymore. And when I did, I got little more than a few grunts and demands that I behave and stick to the rules.

"Agreed," Ro echoed, his voice the right amount of quiet and stern. I was usually the troublemaker of the two of us, so I beamed at him with approval. Clearly he was just as fed up with Cy's secrecy and avoidance as I was.

Cyrus hurried along into an open field, hobbling slightly. The pace he was setting was a bit too much for his injury and my belly filled with concern that he would push himself too far. We watched from afar, behind a cluster of trees while Seamus joined him, along with a few other protectors I hadn't encountered during our stay here. Even from our distance, I could practically feel the nervous hum of energy buzzing around them all. Where had all of these protectors come from so suddenly and why the hell were they meeting out here in the middle of the night?

Just beyond them, was a large truck, the engine lulling quietly as if waiting for something. Izzy pulled us further into the forest, away from the bath of light the headlights carved through the trees. The air was layered with a sense of foreboding and urgency —so much so that I could feel individual hairs standing up on my arms.

"Do you know those other protectors?" I asked, belatedly smiling in thanks for her quick thinking.

She nodded, her grey eyes focused hard in their direction. It was impressive, the way that she could turn off her typically giddy personality and trade it in for such extreme diligence. "That's Barn," she pointed to a tall Black man, lined with lean muscles and a quiet strength. "He's one of Headmistress Alleva's bondmates. She must finally be back from her trip."

A shudder ran through me, imagining Alleva as a more adult, more powerful version of her daughter, Reza. Of everyone I'd met at The Guild, Reza seemed to hate me the most. Almost every time we'd interacted, she'd drenched me in vitriol and made it abundantly clear that she didn't think I belonged here. She was also ridiculously attached to Atlas, so I wasn't surprised that they shared an opinion of me.

I just wished that the opinion was a pleasant one.

Hopefully Alleva was more tolerable, or at least didn't hate me as much as her daughter seemed to. Because while Reza was mostly harmless, I had a feeling her mother could legitimately make my life miserable if she wanted to.

The man, Barn was glaring at Cyrus, an unreadable expression on his face. Judging from the rigidity in his posture, and the way his face was scrunched up as if he'd just consumed something from a sewer, it wasn't a pleasant emotion rolling through his body.

Which was weird. I was used to most people I'd met around

The Guild fawning over Cy, so it was particularly strange to see him looked on with such bridled anger.

"What's his deal with Cyrus?" Ro asked, giving voice to my own curiosity.

Izzy shook her head briefly before looking at us, her brows turned down in thought. "I don't know. And there are a few protectors out there that I don't actually know. I think I've seen one in passing down in the research labs, but I don't know her name. They might be transients who operate in one of the smaller bases. There's a handful scattered throughout the country, and even bigger bases on other continents. Alleva was visiting the one in South America."

I opened my mouth to ask another question, curious about the politics and systems of power operating throughout the world with various guilds, but a sudden, strong blast of air flattened the grass around them. Looking up, I saw a large plane descending, and noticed for the first time a long, paved runway a few hundred feet away from the crowd gathered in the field. Was this one of the planes that was used for missions?

We waited silently, tension pulsing around us, while the plane descended. My breathing was coming out steady and slow, which was odd considering my heart was hammering against my ribcage with excitement. The side door opened and I watched as a lean, hourglass figure came running down the steps, waving her hands towards Cyrus's group.

Declan.

My spirits lifted at the sight of her, happy to see that Six was back. But that excitement disappeared almost as soon as it arrived. Her bright eyes were like small flashing orbs in the distance, and I could tell from the strain in her stance that something was wrong.

Declan was always more serious and reserved than most of the protectors and students I'd encountered here, but something about the energy unfolding around her seemed so much more so now.

Suddenly, an unexplainable need to see the other members of the team went through me in deep waves. What had happened out there?

My hands gripped tightly into rough bark, and I watched as Atlas, Declan, and Eli carried a stretcher down the stairs. Their steps were hurried and determined. Even from this far away, I could practically feel the fear coursing through them all. A realization alone that nearly destroyed me. They weren't a fearful group.

"Can you see who that is?" Ro asked, his neck craning slightly as he swept a few stray strands of hair from his eyes. Izzy pulled him back. He'd stepped over the tree line and if any of the group looked our way, he would be visible.

"No," she said, "but stay hidden. This looks bad and we really shouldn't be here. Punishment at The Guild can be quite...intense. Everyone has a place, and this is not ours. And insubordination can be dealt with ruthlessly."

Her typical upbeat demeanor disappeared almost instantly, and I watched as an intelligent focus washed over her. She was in protector mode and I knew immediately that she would be a force to be reckoned with on missions. Not for the first time, I wished desperately to be on her team when we graduated. She ducked low, her head tilted in focus—it was like her mind was running a mile a minute, studying every detail in the group.

"This is bad," she whispered with a small, indiscernible shake of her head. "Sharla mentioned earlier that they were due to check in hours ago but didn't. Something went really, really wrong. Atlas's group is known for finishing tasks on time, early even. They either broke protocol or encountered more trouble than they were expecting."

Scanning the crowd, I waited for one more familiar body, but after the pilot descended, radio in hand, I realized no one else was leaving the plane.

"It's Wade," I whispered, my heart dropping into my stomach. Something drew me towards the group, a desperate need to make sure that Wade was okay, and I had to physically ground my body to keep from running out there to check on him.

We watched as they rushed Wade through the open doors of the truck, Declan and Eli hopping in to join him. Atlas stayed back, though I watched as his steady eyes followed his team until the vehicle was almost completely out of sight. He was huddled in deep conversation with Cyrus and the other protectors, a thick tension encasing them all.

My focus was caught between the disappearing truck and worry for Wade, and a deep desire to hear what Atlas was telling them. I wanted desperately to know what had happened on their mission, and I wanted desperately to know that Wade was okay. It took a lot to kill or even seriously injure a protector, and something about the heaviness rolling through the group told me that Wade was in trouble. This wasn't a run-of-the-mill scratch. Unlike Ro's mission with Ten, It was clear that Atlas and his team definitely encountered whichever supernatural beast they were hunting.

Cyrus and Seamus led the group towards the opening of the woods, a few dozen feet away from our hiding spot. We fell back deeper into the shadows of the trees, the three of us collectively holding our breath. Atlas trailed behind, his shoulders stiff and angular. Wade was his brother. Why wasn't he the one in the truck with him? If it were the same situation and Ro was the injured one, not even Cyrus could keep me from his bedside. But the Atlas standing bathed in the moonlight seemed different from the one I was used to, broken somehow, like a shadow of his usual self.

As soon as the thought filtered through my mind, Atlas's dark eyes met mine, the fear settling on his face turning to anger.

"Shit," Izzy muttered, her eyes widening with fear.

We were busted.

3
MAX

Luckily, Atlas didn't say anything and he didn't seem to rat us out to anyone with the power to punish us. His dark eyes trailed over us, his head shaking almost imperceptibly before he followed the rest of the group. If I didn't know better, it almost seemed like he was warning us to stay back, to stay hidden.

Izzy, Ro, and I waited silently for a solid half hour, discussing the possibilities of what happened and hoping like hell that Atlas kept our spying to himself. I wouldn't hold my breath though, he didn't seem like the type to offer an unrequited favor. We made our way quietly back to the dorms, each of us lost in our own thoughts about what we'd just witnessed. Izzy left us for her rooms with a promise that she'd get in touch with Sharla to see if she could find out about what had happened. Ro and I were determined to wait for Cyrus. He wasn't answering his phone and hadn't shown up at his room.

After an hour of wearing a path through my rug pacing around, Ro convinced me to try and sleep, promising that we'd find out what happened in the morning. Wherever Cyrus was, it was clear that he was busy and that filling us in on the happenings of the night was low on his to-do list.

For once, I actually listened. Or at least I tried to. I focused all of my energy on willing my eyes shut and switching my brain off for several hours. But at two in the morning, I gave up. I threw on a pair of leggings and a dark tank, dragging the nurse's keycard I'd swiped from inside my pillow case. In the days since my recovery, she hadn't come looking for it, nor had she asked for it back, so I assumed it was as good as mine now. And if not, it was easier to ask for forgiveness than permission in this instance.

And then, with as much stealth as I could muster, I left my room and then our apartment suite, determined to find Wade or at the very least, one of the members of his team. For a moment, I was tempted to wake Ro so that I'd have company, but the soft snores echoing through his door convinced me to leave him be. He'd been sleeping so little since I returned from the infirmary, constantly worrying about my own health at the expense of his own.

I could wait until morning, sure, but the thought of Wade lying hurt in the hospital wing, or something unspeakably worse than simply hurt, was plaguing my mind. I couldn't wait a second more to make sure that he was okay. It was like a weird, invisible string was pulling behind my ribs, insisting that I check up on him tonight.

The halls were largely empty, and I only passed one of the professors, I think her name was Margie, patrolling in the east wing. I hid quickly in an empty classroom, counting the seconds until the click-clack of her footsteps turned down another hall and then, eventually, disappeared altogether. Students didn't really have a strict curfew or anything, but I had a feeling that roaming the halls alone in the middle of the night was at the very least deeply frowned upon.

I'd only ever snuck out once before while living with Cyrus, and he had been waiting for me in the kitchen, a silent look of disappointment coloring his face, when I eventually returned. I was grounded for two weeks, unable to watch movies or read any books—and seeing as we lived on our own, with very little to keep ourselves occupied, the punishment was heavy enough that I swore never to repeat the crime.

Until now.

Banking on the hope that the rest of The Guild didn't keep tabs on the protectors with quite as much vigilance as Cyrus had, I made my way to the infirmary doors in less than fifteen minutes. The doors were unlocked. I pressed my fingers around the cool handles, pulling the heavy frame open. I moved the door carefully, trying to be as silent and slow as possible. With a deep breath, I gave one final tug, hoping that I wouldn't meet any angry faces when the door swung fully open.

A single, buzzing light lit the main hall, a guard snoring softly at the front desk. His ankles were crossed, feet rising above the table. A car magazine had slipped slightly, revealing a beaten up book resting open on his chest. A beautiful girl with disproportionate features was pictured on the front, her shirt pulled seductively low. A tall, lumberjack-looking man was standing behind her, his large palm resting possessively on her hip. I bit back a grin, picturing the muscular guard secretly perusing romance novels in the library before his shift. People could be so unpredictable sometimes.

I slowly peeled off my sneakers, hoping to muffle my steps slightly, before walking along the hall. The first two rooms were empty, the third filled with a girl around my age, maybe a few years older, sleeping soundly. When I got to the fourth door, I bit back my surprise, finding Wade passed out, looking beaten and worn against the harsh white of the hospital sheets. Something about him seemed to be missing, like his body was absent of the deep glow I'd come to admire. I waited one long, painstaking moment to see if he was breathing, and exhaled harshly in relief when the sheets surrounding him lifted up and back down with his lungs.

Throwing caution aside, I opened the door and shuffled quickly to his side. My eyes catalogued him head-to-toe, recognizing his dark, cropped hair and features that were somehow both soft and sharp. His usually tawny skin was significantly paler than I remembered, and covered with several fresh wounds. My heartbeat quickened when I realized that he was shirtless, and I blushed, suddenly feeling guilty for trespassing during his sleep. Something seemed so intimate about standing here above him, studying him as he slumbered.

Trying desperately to ignore the lean muscles covering his torso, I studied a large bandage covering both his neck and his side. It was unusual for a protector to have so many unhealed wounds. It had been several hours since Six arrived back from their mission and I half expected to find Wade bouncing up and down, rearing to get back to his own room like I had been.

To see him so frail and beaten up, so long after his return...

My fingers itched, like they wanted nothing more than to smooth the small crease between his brows, to peel back the bandages and check the wounds myself. Of all the members of Six, Wade had been the sweetest, the most accommodating and welcoming in his own quiet way. The night before the mission, he'd spent so much time, given so much patience, answering my questions about the culture and rules at The Guild. Whereas Atlas, and although to a lesser extent, even the rest of his team, made me feel like a nuisance, an obligation, Wade was genuinely warm and welcoming. There was a weird electricity between us, like we were drawn together in some inexplicable way.

I needed to know what had happened to him. Forcing myself to look away from his prone form, I searched the machines plugged into him for clues. One of them was beeping with a steady, slow pulse, but I didn't know enough about the tools being used here, or protector physiology, to have any idea what it meant. The machines surrounding him looked completely different from the ones I was used to seeing in human medical dramas and I wondered, briefly, how different the technology here was from the sort that humans used.

My hands reached towards the side table, noticing a bag of

his things. Just as my fingers were about to make contact, eager to see if there were any clues on his personal items about what he'd been through, I jumped back, barely swallowing the squeal that tried desperately to leave my mouth.

Atlas.

He was sitting in a chair a few feet away from Wade's bed, fast asleep. His left foot was crossed at his right knee, his hands folded around a large, imposing knife, like he was stationed as protection over his brother. What sort of threat did he anticipate meeting here? Or did he always rest like this, perpetually prepared for doom and gloom?

I breathed a sigh of relief when I realized he was asleep. Unable to pass up the opportunity to see him without his characteristic scowl, I studied him. His dark hair, which was usually stylishly tossed around, was even messier now, sticking up in various directions like he'd been running his fingers through it. Small lines marred his forehead, his face intense and commanding even in sleep.

Glancing down his face, I noticed dried blood splotches on one cheek, and then more on each arm. I wasn't sure whether or not the blood belonged to him—if it did, the wounds were long closed now—but it was clear he hadn't bothered cleaning up after the mission. My chest constricted, warmed by the realization that he must have been worried sick about Wade.

I could empathize. If Ro were the one in here, I'd be absolutely beside myself. Maybe Atlas wasn't quite as heartless as he let on.

I wondered how many people he'd threatened in order to be allowed to stay for the night. When I was down here, my nurse Greta had forcefully kicked everyone out, not allowing even Ro to stay by my side. My lips pulled up at the thought of her trying to boss Atlas around.

Satisfied that Wade was at the very least alive, I started walking backwards towards the door. There wasn't any more information to learn tonight, no evidence that I could quietly gather to try and piece together what happened. And truthfully, I'd rather be caught down here by even a scowling Greta—anyone really—than Atlas. Something told me that if he was willing to let my spying slide once tonight, he absolutely would not be willing to extend the same favor again. Especially not when he was in such a vulnerable state as he was now, resting at his brother's side.

My socks slid smoothly across the floor, and I studied Atlas's almost-but-not-quite-relaxed face as I migrated towards the door.

And I reached it successfully too.

The problem was that as my fingers gripped the smooth handle, a door in the close distance slammed shut, bringing unfamiliar voices into the hallway.

"Do they think he'll survive?" one voice asked, squeaky with a failed attempt at whispering.

"I don't know," the second responded, clipped and far more successful at keeping the volume down.

"Medical staff seems torn."

"I have a feeling that Tarren will pull Atlas out of here if he doesn't make it," replied the second speaker.

I strained, pressing my ear greedily against the cool metal door, trying desperately to hear the rest of the conversation as the two protectors made their way down the far end of the hall. Who was Tarren? What did they mean by pull Atlas out of here? Out of The Guild? And, more importantly, was the staff really torn on whether or not Wade would make it? I couldn't imagine anyone else mattering so much to Atlas's future, so it must've been him they were discussing.

My stomach dropped suddenly, and I forced myself to ignore them. Wade would survive this. He had to.

Resisting the urge to look back once more at Atlas and Wade, I twisted the doorknob as slowly as possible, a breath of relief parting my lips when the door cracked open without a sound.

Carefully, I pulled it open, a few inches at a time until, all at once, it was forced closed again with a dull, resounding snap.

Heart pounding, I turned around, finding myself caged against the door by a very awake, very angry Atlas.

For a few moments, he was silent, studying me with dark eyes that were ringed with an almost gold color. The gold seemed to practically glow as he studied me. His skin was drawn, paler than usual, made more noticeable by the dark, scratchy stubble lining his cheeks and chin. Even in exhaustion, coated by worry for his brother, he still looked beautiful. It was infuriating. I watched the way the muscles in his jaw clenched, and could almost hear the sound of his teeth grinding together.

Reminding myself to breathe, I pressed back against the door, desperate to put some space between us. Only thing was that the doors were, well, super solid, and there was nowhere for me to go.

Panic rang through my ears as I waited desperately for Atlas to say something, or at the very least for my own mouth to gain enough courage to open. Something seemed so fragile in the moment, so feral about his stare; like if I didn't say the right thing, he would pounce and tear me limb from limb, enjoying every second of it.

"I—um," I started, before snapping my jaw closed again. Speechless was a new experience for me.

The gold threading through his dark irises was mesmerizing up close, and I felt a weird compulsion to reach out and cup his cheek, to feel the press of his stubble against my palm. Atlas tilted his head slightly, slanting his eyes, not unlike a cat closing in on its prey.

He wouldn't actually kill me right? They had to have rules against that sort of thing here.

I hoped so anyway. If not, they needed to make some and quick.

With one more desperate breath and silent pep talk, I met

his eyes. I was the intruder here, he had every right to an explanation.

"I'm sorry. I didn't mean to wake you." I wasn't sure whether or not he'd heard the two protectors speaking; it was unclear how long he'd been awake. "I just, I needed to check on Wade. I had to know he was okay and Cyrus hadn't come to alert us. And we couldn't track him down, which is unusual enough for a guy like Cyrus. I'm used to him being around when I need him." I looked around at the violently white room that seemed to almost glow, even in the cold darkness. "I know I'm new here, but Wade has been really welcoming and helpful, especially my first few days with getting me on track with Guild history and trying to come to terms with the culture shock. I tried sleeping, really I did, but I couldn't shut my eyes for more than two seconds without worrying about—"

One long, thin finger pressed harshly to my lips, setting a pulse of electricity down my spine.

"I, er, uh—" I started again, mumbling awkwardly against his pointer finger. At a low growl that rumbled low in his throat, I stopped.

As soon as I was no longer stuttering and stumbling over my words, I heard the soft click of heavy shoes coming down the hall again.

Had he heard them so far off in the distance before I did? I knew protectors came into their senses more fully after turning nineteen, but still.

"Eighth one this month." It was voice two again. They must've been making rounds, or dropping something off; they were heading back towards the direction they'd originally come from.

"I know, and that's only in the western half of the country. I've heard it's been just as bad on the east coast as well," voice one whisper-yelled. "Will be interesting to hear about Alleva's trip and if things are as bad there as they are here. I hope for all of our sakes that they aren't."

The owner of voice two said something else, but it was garbled and I couldn't make out the words, not with my heart pounding heavily at the close proximity of Atlas.

His dark eyes stared straight through mine, like he was off tracing his own winding thoughts and not really looking at me. I watched the pools of brown glistening with intelligence. Something was running through his head, I just didn't understand what. I had a feeling that Atlas was the type of person I'd never be able to fully read, the type of person no one could ever fully read.

I did, however, suddenly realize that his finger was still pressed against my lips—a realization that brought a deep warmth to my cheeks. I prayed that he couldn't feel the heat, that he didn't realize the effect his proximity was having on me. It was suddenly impossible to look him in the eye, every part of my body tingling with awareness of how very, very close we were together. My lips parted briefly, my tongue a centimeter away from making contact with his finger before I swallowed, unsure of how to have a conversation with him like this. There was nowhere for me to go, no way for me to create space between us. Suddenly I desperately needed breathing room.

As if realizing the same thing, he brought his hand roughly down to his side and took several steps back.

"Do you think the rules of The Guild don't apply to you, Bentley?" His voice was even more gravelly than usual, an edge that wasn't typically there. Was it sleep or anger changing it?

"It's not that, I just needed to know that Wade was okay," I said, straightening my spine slightly. I didn't regret coming down to check on him, no matter how angry Atlas was or how much trouble I was going to get into. I couldn't explain it, not really, not even to myself. I just knew that I couldn't sleep until I knew that he was alive.

"And earlier," he said, opening and closing his right fist like he had to restrain from attacking, "what's your excuse for then?"

Curiosity? There really wasn't an excuse. I just wanted to

know what had Cyrus all panicky. I bit softly at my bottom lip, stalling. I was unsure of what to say, fully aware that no answer would be a reason good enough for Atlas. He was angry, and I could tell from his expression that he was determined to direct it at me no matter what.

Ultimately, I decided to just ignore Atlas's question and focus on my own. "Wade, what happened to him?"

"That's not your concern." His words were clipped, eyes like ice. "Students aren't cleared for learning the details of private missions, especially not students who have been involved in our world for a grand total of one week."

It had been slightly more than a week, but I didn't think this was the time to argue on that point. I met his eyes, unwilling to be bullied on this. "Fine. I don't need to know the details of the mission. Just tell me—is Wade going to be alright? I need—I need to know, okay?"

I wasn't sure whether or not I was imaging it, but the corners of Atlas's eyes seemed to soften, ever so slightly. He looked over at Wade, and my stomach dropped a bit. Atlas was worried. For some reason that, more than anything, had fear gripping at my insides with a vengeance. He wasn't the type to get worried. When he was worried, that meant that everyone needed to be worried.

"I don't—I don't know," he said on a heavy exhale. There was a dejection about him all of a sudden, and I could practically hear the concern dripping from his words. I felt chilled more than anything, to the bone. Atlas looked scared, vulnerable even, in a way that was completely antithetical to who he was. I'd only known him for a short while, I knew that. But still, even I knew that this was bad.

We both stood silently for what felt like an hour, but for what was probably just a few minutes, neither of us able to look away from Wade's sleeping form. We both silently watched the steady rise and fall of his chest, his breath beating an atypical cadence.

29

Life as a protector was difficult and short-lived—Cyrus had never been shy about making sure we knew that. In fact, I was fairly certain that was half the reason he wanted to keep us away from this world for as long as he could. Until, that is, the supernatural world started coming after us and we lost the luxury of hiding from it. Ro and I had talked many times about the odds of us both surviving past our fifties. Like most protectors, we'd come to terms with the idea that we'd go down fighting while we were still in our prime—it was a point of honor for most of our kind. Still, I wasn't ready to accept that fate for Wade, not for any of the people that I cared about or had collected as friends recently.

Steeling myself, I turned away from Wade, eyes locking on Atlas again. "He will be okay, Atlas."

I hoped so, anyway. Desperately.

I breathed in and out, steadying myself. "I know he will."

I didn't.

Atlas met my gaze and his shoulders dropped, like I'd taken a huge weight off of him, just by choosing to be positive. It was a strange sensation, and I didn't know what to make of the sudden shift between us—a new understanding, maybe?

After a few seconds, lingering in the brief relief, Atlas shook his head. "You should go, Bentley. I won't tell anyone you were down here, but you need to go now. And from now on, you need to follow the rules. No more butting into things that don't concern you. Insubordination is how people get hurt," he glanced towards his brother again, almost unconsciously, "not following protocol gets people killed."

I nodded and, without another word, opened the door and left Atlas alone in the room with his brother.

As soon as I closed the door, I saw through the window that he was moving back to Wade's side. He gripped his brother's hand gently before sliding back into his chair, head ducking low, elbows digging into his thighs. The two of them were so different. I knew that they were only half brothers, but they seemed so opposite, both in appearance and personality. How did that happen?

I found myself desperate to know more about them, curiosity tugging behind my navel like an angry fishhook. What was it about these brothers that drew me in so much? Wade—Wade made sense. He was warm and open, intelligent and kind. But Atlas was all hard edges and cruel lines; the type of guy I should want to distance myself from at all costs.

My curiosity was irrelevant. Atlas had made himself clear, butting into Six matters would get me in a world of trouble and I had enough things to worry about right now.

Slowly, I turned. I would go, yes, but I wasn't going back to bed. Following rules was not going to be one of my strong suits while living in this world. Especially not when I was already down here and had another friend I needed to visit.

4
ATLAS

I closed the door after Max left and fell into the metal frame with all of my weight, relying on it to keep me standing. Watching Wade breathe, his chest rising and falling in erratic patterns felt like torture. We'd lost so much already. I couldn't do this without him here. What was the fucking point?

And I hated the way that she made me forget, for just one second, what I was and what had happened. Her scent lingered in the room, and I breathed through my mouth to keep from sinking into it. There was a lull there, a peaceful promise of what could be, if things weren't how they were. That way lay danger, so I didn't let myself float in the possibilities for long. There were far more important things to consider.

I sat down next to Wade's bed and grabbed his hand. He'd be okay. And when he woke up, we'd get back to the hunt—we'd get our revenge. This was the second time now that this particular pack of wolves had taken something important from us. It had to be stopped.

And, Max, well—we needed to keep her as far from us as possible. She was pure and good and naive. She didn't belong in The Guild Academy. Hell, she didn't belong in The Guild period. This place would ruin her like it had ruined all of us.

All it did was take.

She needed to go back to that miserable small town she'd come from, whether she wanted to or not. I knew that Cyrus and Seamus had charged us with looking after her, but maybe it was time to convince her to leave, to go back. She wasn't safe here and we weren't able to protect her in the way that they wanted us to. I didn't like the way that my crew responded to her, watching every breath she took. We were all curious about her, and it was going to cost us. We couldn't afford to split our focus, the stakes were just far too high right now.

As soon as I settled my heartrate back down to an acceptable pace, the door flung open with a resounding crash. Cyrus barged in, dark eyes blazing, followed by an equally irate Seamus. Generally Seamus was the more easygoing of the two, but there was an aggressiveness clouding him today that made the brothers look more alike than they generally did.

Cyrus scanned the room, his feral, intelligent eyes taking everything in before they finally settled on Wade. His brows bent down slightly in concern as he took a few steps closer, studying Wade's steady heartbeat along with all of the numbers the machines hooked to him were spitting out. "Max was just here, wasn't she?" He didn't even bother looking at me as he asked the question, though he made it sound more like an observation. "That infernal girl follows rules about as well as an acorn reads."

I sat up, back straight as a rod as I looked towards the door. Had she made it back to her room yet? If she moved quickly, she was probably back, tucked away in her bedroom, lulled into sleep. For some reason, I didn't want to rat her out, didn't want to admit that there was some misguided part of her that was just as drawn to my team members as they were to her. Admitting it would make it real, make it so much more difficult to ignore or brush aside.

"Don't look so shellshocked, boy," Cyrus said, his voice a low grumble that practically sent vibrations through the room. He pressed two lean fingers against Wade's pulse as if he didn't trust the electronic readouts. Curiosity flashed across his features. What did he see that I couldn't? "I know the girl well enough to know she's going around sticking her nose into things. I saw her follow us out to the clearing earlier. I've learned over the years that sometimes it's better to ignore her actions rather than encourage her by straight up telling her no. Insufferably stubborn, that girl."

I frowned, glancing at Seamus. He was studying Cyrus, face dark in thought. For some reason I had a feeling that he was having trouble looking me in the eye. Seamus had been like a father to me, in more ways than my own had. Part of me was shocked that he wasn't offering words of comfort right now. Maybe he was just relieved that Eli wasn't the one sitting here in the bed, unconscious and hooked up to machines. I couldn't blame him. Familial bonds did weird things to you sometimes. Grief was a bitch.

"I sent her back to her room, sir," I mumbled, staring at the steady rise and fall of Wade's chest. I'd never been so focused on someone's breathing before, like I was terrified that at any moment, it would stop. How long would he be out like this?

Cyrus bit back a grin, his eyes lighting up briefly with fondness, or something like it. "I doubt it." He leaned up against the wall, no doubt resting some of the weight off his leg. "If I know her half as well as I think I do, she'll be sneaking down into that damn research lab again, to check on that damn hound. Stubborn, stubborn girl."

Right. In all of the chaos of the past week, I almost forgot about the hellhound. And about the fact that Max seemed hellbent on breaking that thing out of here. The rooms were secure enough that I didn't think her infrequent visits were that big of a concern. It wasn't like she was at risk of being attacked down there, so long as protocol was observed, and the creatures were locked away properly. But still, something about her being down there by herself didn't sit right with me. Maybe Declan's paranoia about the labs was starting to settle over me these days. Shit like that was annoyingly contagious and Declan and I always seemed to be on similar wavelengths.

The hellhound was another thing I needed more information about. Why was it here and why was it so drawn to Max? I could feel curiosity battling with my desire to keep her at arm's length. I cleared my throat, glancing between the two men. "If it would help, my team—we can doctor the footage. That way we can monitor her visits and make sure she doesn't get into trouble." Or at least slightly less trouble than she would be in otherwise.

I wasn't sure why I offered it. Maybe if someone took her stolen key card back and chastised her a few times, she'd learn. The girl needed to fall in line. I wasn't sure that I shared Cyrus's desire to turn the other cheek and pretend to ignore her bad habits.

Cyrus glanced briefly in my direction, an unreadable expression on his face. Truthfully, most of his expressions were unreadable. The guy was a damn vault ninety percent of the time. It was kind of infuriating, if I was being honest.

"That would be ideal. If," he paused, nodding to his brother, "we are all agreed that it's okay to ignore this one minor insurrection?"

Seamus opened his mouth as if to dissent, his hands perched sharply on his hips. It was strange, watching the brothers together. For so much of my life here at Headquarters, Seamus had been top dog. He didn't have to answer to anyone, and he was intimidating in his own right. But Cyrus seemed to have an edge when it came to their decisions.

"I have a feeling that she'll be more likely to follow most of our rules if we let her think she's getting away with just this one thing," Cyrus added, effectively stopping his brother's protest before it even started.

"Fine," Seamus bit out. "But it's on you two to handle. I'm on thin ice as it is, so I can't be bothered taking risks on something so superficial." He turned to me, arching a single brow. "I'm sorry son, I know you're probably exhausted, but we need to go over what happened out there."

Right. We had discussed the basics over the phone on the flight back, and even more briefly upon our arrival. But the time between finding Wade and running into Max had felt almost like a daze, like I was there, experiencing the events, but also like I wasn't. What had I already reported on? What more was there?

I was silent for a long, stretched moment, thinking back over the night. "Like I mentioned before, we saw a group of vampires and werewolves working together. There were at least ten. We think Wade took on four solo, as impossible as that sounds, and Dec and I had the other six. It's possible there were more but—" I choked back anxiety, remembering that room bathed in blood and corpses, Wade impossibly still. I needed to call our father, but I wanted desperately to wait until Wade woke up, until I had positive news to share. Calling him would signal a shift, a shift I was desperate to avoid as long as possible. Breathing deeply, I focused back on the two men before me. "When we found Wade, we couldn't stay to explore. His situation was dire," I cleared my throat and shook the haziness from my thoughts, "obviously."

Generally, we were supposed to bring back any of our conquests, dead or alive—although ideally alive. The beasts in the labs were brought here by different team missions, it was how we learned about the creatures in the hell realm, how we found their weaknesses. And this batch of monsters would have been particularly useful. Especially since, if my research was correct, I was quite certain it was the pack of wolves that had taken down Sarah.

And now that they were working with other species, they were even more valuable for study. If it had been anyone else, anyone but Wade, I probably would have followed protocol. Stuck around for those extra few minutes, to try and collect at least a specimen or two. But in that moment, all I could see was red, my every thought clouded by fear that he wouldn't make it.

Every moment counted. And his life would take precedence. Every single time.

"I'm sorry," I added, and I meant it. I would have liked to be the sort of protector capable of turning off, of being capable of that sort of emotional numbing. It was invaluable in this line of work. But I wasn't that protector, not anymore. I'd been watching over Wade for as long as I could remember. It was the one consistency in my life. He was my weakness in a world where it was important to have none.

Seamus reached over to me, softly squeezing my shoulder. I blinked, choking back any emotion whirling in my gut. It was such a paternal gesture, filled with a sort of understanding and forgiveness that I wasn't used to from my own father.

"It's okay, son. I would have done the same thing if it were Eli. If it were any of you." He exhaled sharply, glancing towards Cyrus, the room momentarily filled with nothing but the soft beeps and whirls of the machines. They were comforting in their own way. "But we need to know any information you have. This is the first we've heard of different species working together like this. Vamps and wolves especially, they're generally so territorial. There have been so many shifts recently that it feels like we're constantly behind the curve, trying to figure out each situation as it changes. And then there's Wade."

I looked back at my brother, his smooth, brown skin clear now that the staff had washed away most of the stray streaks of blood. If I allowed myself, momentarily I could pretend that he was just asleep.

"They're not sure what's wrong with him," Cyrus said as he ran a large hand through his unruly mop of hair. "He's just...unconscious. Vitals are mostly normal, considering the blood loss. We just have to hope that he wakes up and, if he does, we go from there. It's highly unusual and we're at a bit of an impasse."

I bristled at the way he said 'if,' as if he was convinced it wouldn't happen, that Wade would be in a coma forever or else slowly slip away, halfway to ghosthood. Supernatural bites were unpredictable a lot of the time, but I'd never heard of them doing this, pushing the protector into an odd, sleep-like daze, as if frozen or suspended in time.

"Either way," Seamus said, letting out an exasperated, hollow sigh, "what happened today changes everything."

5
MAX

I grabbed the keycard I'd swiped during my first visit to the infirmary from the pocket in the waistband of my legging—seriously, whoever came up with legging with pockets and zippered compartments was a freaking genius—and made my way down the familiar path, determined to see Ralph before I let myself fall asleep for the night. Luckily, the two protectors on night duty were nowhere in sight, having already completed their rounds, so I made my way to the supernatural menagerie with little trouble.

When I crept up to Ralph's cage in the far corner of the dark room, he whimpered softly—a sad, empty sort of sound—and I watched as his tail lifted an inch before falling again. He seemed so much smaller, so much more defeated since the last time I'd been here. Even his lustrous black hair seemed duller somehow. I felt my eyes blur with moisture.

"Ralph," I said, racing to press my palm against the glass, as if I could pet him or comfort him through it, "what happened to you?"

He whined again and managed a soft lick where my hand was pressed, a gesture that shattered my heart into pieces.

A harsh laugh echoed behind me and I turned abruptly,

coming face-to-face with the vampire from before. He was sitting in a cross-legged position, his unusual eyes—one gold, one dark brown—studying me. I shivered under his scrutiny, drawn to him and repulsed for being so. We hadn't learned much about vampire compulsion, but I'd bet money this one was a master of it. Vampires were predators, built to be beautiful and lethal. Everything about them was designed to draw their victims in. And this one, well, I had a feeling he was more lethal than most.

"What do you think happened to him, little protector? Protectors happened to him. The Guild happened to him. This place is designed for misery and pain for creatures like us." The playful, almost teasing tone the vampire had last time I was down here now felt harsh and angry, his words jagged and dripping with fury.

I bristled when he said the word 'us,' as if Ralph was anything like him. Ralph, who was giant and gentle? Granted, I didn't know the hellhound well at all, but I could feel it in my bones that he was safe, warm. And this vampire seemed as far from safe as you could get.

"But I was told they were simply running tests." I looked back at Ralph. He was sitting up now, and I could tell that he was using all of his energy to try and greet me. In my mind, that had meant a few blood draws, maybe some scans. Nothing quite so debilitating. "Tests shouldn't leave him this —exhausted."

The vampire laughed again, the strangely musical sound filtered through a hollow growl. "Do you trust everything the protectors tell you?"

"Seamus wouldn't lie," I answered, my chin lifting slightly. I wanted desperately to believe that. "He assured me and Cyrus that Ralph would be safe, that he would be unharmed." And Cyrus had promised the same. I couldn't stomach the thought of him lying to me. He'd kept his fair share of secrets, sure, but he never lied unless it was to protect us. I wouldn't allow myself to consider that he knew what was going on down here, that he knew how completely drained Ralph was.

"Believe what you want, little protector. But they don't care about the hound. They've been running him ragged, hooking him up to all sorts of machines, and keeping him under heavy sedation." The vampire ran a hand lazily through his wavy, platinum hair, swiping it out of his eyes. I wondered how long he'd been locked up in here, how he was captured and who captured him. There was a stillness about him that unsettled me, like even though he was the one inside a cage, I was the one being closely studied. I shook my head, bringing my focus back to the current issue. The only issue.

What were they testing Ralph for? I didn't want to believe a word the vamp was saying, but that explained the slow movements and the glazed look in Ralph's dark eyes. He'd seemed so aware, so intelligent when I was down here last. Now he appeared tranquil and like he was living in a haze.

I opened my mouth, glancing between Ralph and the vampire, and then closed it again. I wanted to stand up for the protectors, to stand up for The Guild and my people, but the words wouldn't leave my lips, no matter how much I tried to mold them. I was a protector, but I was also like a spectator, observing from the outside without really understanding.

The vampire was standing up now, studying me with rapt attention. I could tell from the smug look on his face that he was pleased I was lost for words. He enjoyed controlling the situation and my reactions to it.

"Hellhounds are rare," he continued, tilting his head as he spoke. His mismatched eyes shone with a apathetic intelligence that sent shivers down my spine. "I doubt the protectors have ever had one under their scrutiny before. They almost never enter this realm, and when they do, none who wish them harm live to act on it. It's very curious, really. Why would a hellhound be so interested in a female protector? Why allow himself to get captured and tortured, just to be in her vicinity?"

41

Guilt churned low in my belly. This infuriating vampire was right. Ralph was here because of me. He'd allowed himself to be captured because he wanted to make sure I was safe. I didn't know why the hellhound was acting as my guardian, but I'd do anything to sever the connection if it would help him escape and get back to his own world.

"I don't understand," I said, my voice soft, almost a whisper. I knew that I should ignore him, that listening to a monster was a terrible idea. Even entertaining the idea of a conversation with such a creature was a terrible idea. But still, as I brought my eyes up to meet the vampire's, I took an unintentional step closer to him. "Ralph—he's not evil. He hasn't harmed anyone. He's saved a protector. He's not like the other realm beasts."

The vampire's jaw tightened at that last sentence, before going preternaturally still. I had a feeling that if there wasn't magic glass separating us, My head would now be separated from my spine.

After a long, terrifying moment in which I couldn't even force myself to breathe, we watched each other. Then, just before I felt like the tension between us would explode, he took a step back into his own cage, the darkness shadowing him slightly. "Yes, of course. Because all other realm beasts are evil."

I was inching closer and closer towards the vampire, until I was mere feet away from the glass separating us. It suddenly seemed so tenuous, so fragile, and I shivered at the thought of it shattering. My hand unconsciously feathered against the bitten spot on my neck, all remnants now long healed. Something deep down told me that where the other vampire had failed at breaking me, this one would succeed if given the opportunity.

With a sigh, he shook his head softly, like I'd disappointed him somehow. It was odd, to feel like I'd disappointed a creature so evil and dangerous. As soon as the mood crossed my mind, I shook it away, unwilling to dissect it.

"You'd do well to question the world you're living in, Max

Bentley." His voice was callous and cold, all teasing dissolved from his tone.

The fragile moment between us snapped immediately, and my eyes pierced his—he was too far back into the darkness now for me to see them clearly, but I remembered the vividness of his one dark eye and one golden eye to picture them clearly enough. "How do you know my name?"

His lips curved slowly, briefly revealing the soft, white points of his canines as they shifted from his gums. I shivered and had a feeling he enjoyed making me uncomfortable. He tilted his head before turning his back to me. "You should go. Don't believe everything you are told here, little protector. And trust no one." His words grew so soft I couldn't be sure whether it was him or my imagination that uttered a final "especially me."

I heard the now familiar voices of the two guards who'd almost caught me outside of Wade's room. With a last look and farewell to Ralph, I left and made my way back towards my room. One thing was certain—I was getting Ralph out of there sooner rather than later. And if Cyrus and Seamus wouldn't help, I'd do it myself.

❦

For the first time in as long as I could remember, I was angry with Cyrus. After confronting him in the morning about Ralph's treatment, he more or less ignored me, insisting that he'd handle the situation as soon as he was able. And then he dodged every question I asked about Wade and what happened with their mission, demanding that I stay out of team business until given express directions otherwise. Without another word, he'd brushed me off and joined Seamus for meals. For the next several days, he'd kept vigil outside of our suite for part of the night, like he knew I would try to visit Ralph again. He was always strict when we were growing up, but never cruel. Keeping Ro and me so in the dark since our arrival was starting to dance dangerously close to cruel.

After I filled Ro in though, he was fully on team Ralph and we were knee-deep in trying to plan my hellhound's prison escape. That said, since we were both still extremely green in protector and Guild life, we hadn't exactly gotten very far with our plans.

"I'll see if I can learn more about the research side of things from Sharla and her team," Izzy said, perking up and happy to be included in our plans. Unlike Cyrus, Izzy was more than willing to listen to my concerns and complaints. When I finally came clean to her about Ralph and what really went down the night of my vamp attack, she was so excited to be included that she instantly forgave me for not telling her the truth immediately. And, like Ro, she was hellbent on helping us get Ralph out of there, no questions asked.

The three of us stretched, preparing for our first sparring matches of the day. We'd taken to primarily fighting each other and the members of Ten. After spending so much of my life fighting Ro, it was invigorating to be exposed to everyone's different strengths and weaknesses. I could feel my strategies strengthening each day as I studied individual partners. My body felt like a sponge, absorbing every new move and matching with the best response.

"I haven't heard too much about what goes on in the research area," I said, bouncing on the balls of my feet to get my blood flowing. "Why don't we learn more about it in class?"

Izzy frowned slightly, considering as she squared off with us. "Yeah, that's pretty standard. The research portion of The Guild is the one I'm least familiar with. They don't really tell us much about it as students and you have to have extreme security clearance to get a position down there. But I'll do some digging. Jer's dad is actually pretty high up, so maybe he'll have some insight. He's our best chance for learning more without actually being recruited into their work."

I beamed at her, happy that she was so willing to help, even if it meant bending some rules and protocols. In the meantime, it was decided that I'd devote myself to the company line as much as possible, at least for now. Long enough to get Cyrus off my back and long enough for me to convince people to divulge info about The Guild without fear of me breaking more rules. Ro would do the same.

I ducked my head when Ro threw a relatively sharp punch. Our sparring form wasn't great, since we were mostly using it as smoke and mirrors for our conversation. But I'd been so lost in thought that I'd almost allowed him to get a hit on me—something that hadn't happened much since arriving here. I wasn't sure if it was because of the extra training sessions, but I could feel myself getting better at anticipating attacks, and where the wins between me and Ro used to be pretty split, they were now resoundingly in my favor.

"Dammit," he muttered, bouncing back on the balls of his feet, fists raised. "Almost had you on that one."

Atlas passed us, frowning briefly before studying Izzy and Ro's form. He corrected Ro's posture, redistributing his weight and center of gravity a bit, before moving towards another group.

I could feel the muscles in my jaw tightening as I watched him.

Atlas had gone back to ignoring me since the clandestine meeting in Wade's room. I'd pestered him and Eli to no avail, trying to get an update on Wade's condition, but Six seemed to have a new philosophy: ignore Max at all costs. They'd even left me to spar with Ro and the members of Ten most days, rather than resuming their surveillance of our training. It was odd and I was uncomfortable with the new dynamics. Silly me to assume that Atlas and I had made any progress in our bonding over Wade's condition. If anything, things seemed to be going in the opposite direction.

Eli though, that was new for me. He was the flirtiest of the bunch and so it was especially strange that he was suddenly brushing me off. His generally warm temperament had cooled significantly and while Seamus was as welcoming as ever to me and Ro, Eli had backed off.

While I didn't necessarily miss the overly flirtatious banter, it rubbed me the wrong way that his demeanor had changed so much. And I wasn't entirely sure what I'd done to facilitate or deserve it.

I watched them both weave around fighters, adjusting here, observing there, and let out a long exhale. I could see the exhaustion carving across their expressions, both Eli and Atlas had a worn tension around their eyes.

All at once, I felt like an ass. This probably had nothing to do with me. They were worried about Wade, worried about their teammate. And while he was below fighting off the remnants of whichever creatures he'd encountered, the rest of his team was supposed to go back to work as if nothing happened.

It seemed so cruel, so callous. If I were either of them, I wouldn't want some random new girl pestering me with questions either. With a steady breath, I promised to back off too, to not take their detachment so personally. For now, I knew that Wade's condition hadn't changed. That would be enough for now. It had to be.

Izzy cleared her throat, and I jumped up to avoid Ro's low kick before turning to her. Everyone in the gym was still and staring just beyond us. Ro and I were the only two still fully invested in the session.

"What? Did I miss something?" I asked, wiping the stray hairs out of my eyes. I was coated in sweat, gross. Izzy's lip tweaked briefly into a grin before she nodded her head behind us.

I spun around to see what the big deal was. At the large entryway doors, Cyrus was standing next to Seamus, the two of them together drawing most of the room's attention. And I could understand why, could suddenly see what others saw when they looked at the two brothers. They were imposing dudes. Seeing them together, I was struck again by how much they looked alike. Cyrus was clearly the older by a few years, and he didn't have nearly as warm of a disposition as Seamus, but they were both imposing and slightly terrifying if you didn't know any better. Hell, maybe even if you did know better—I'd grown up with Cyrus and he still sort of terrified me every now and again.

Catching his dark eyes, my stomach clenched with guilt and I broke eye contact. I wasn't used to holding a grudge and it was uncomfortable staying frustrated with him. When you grew up only having two people in your whole world, you did everything you could to keep them close. Since moving here, it seemed like an invisible line had snapped as we all tried to find our place in this new environment. While it was probably healthy for the three of us to have some separation from each other, to branch out, I couldn't help but feel an unwelcome sense of loss.

Maybe if I found a way to bring Cyrus over to team Ralph, it would start to close the distance, just a bit.

"As many of you are aware," Seamus said, his deep voice echoing over the room, the strength he exuded capturing everyone's absolute attention, "attacks in the human world have increased over the last few years, but drastically so over the last few months. We aren't really sure why, but in light of recent...events, we've decided to take some extra precautions for all of our students and to make your training more hands-on. This is, after all, the very thing we are training you for." Seamus glanced briefly at Cyrus and then nodded towards a tall woman who was standing behind them. "Headmistress Alleva and I believe that it is of utmost importance that we get protectors in the academy trained and prepared as quickly as possible, so that we can get you all out there doing your jobs."

Cyrus cleared his throat quietly, but it was a tick I was familiar with—he didn't completely disagree with what Seamus was saying, but he also wasn't completely on board either. I didn't know Seamus well enough yet to read his tells, but I had a feeling that whatever they were about to present us with was the result of some very tense conversations between them.

"And," Seamus added, nodding to Cyrus, "Cyrus and I also believe that the safest way to do that is to pair you up with already successful alpha and beta teams stationed on our campus here."

"Yes, thank you Seamus, I'll take it from here." Headmistress Alleva stepped up next to him, her one bondmate standing on her other side, and I was struck by how uncomfortable Cyrus suddenly looked. To the untrained eye, one which wasn't familiar with all three emotions the man usually showed, nothing looked like it had changed, but I caught the subtle tightening of his muscles, the momentary clench of his right fist. I arched a brow, trying to imagine what Cyrus's life was like before me, before Ro. Where did he fit in this world of protectors and why did he try so hard to leave it—only to return decades later?

Alleva was striking, and looked like an older, more refined version of her daughter. She had straight blond hair, cut into a short bob, with piercingly blue eyes that were so bright they almost looked fake. Her expression screamed no-bullshit and intimidation, but not in an unkind way, like I'd experienced so often with Reza. Alleva looked like she'd seen some shit and pulled herself through it with a quiet, imposing strength. I couldn't help but admire the way she carried herself, rigid posture and all.

Like most protectors around campus, she was dressed head-to-toe in black, but where most of the people I'd encountered were in combat or athletic gear, she was in a pressed suit with crisp, neat lines. She wouldn't have looked out of place in a corporate board meeting, with bone structure that was sharp enough to carve out features in magazines. If she didn't have such a heavy badass energy about her, I would say that she looked out of place in this wide-open gym, filled with sweaty teenagers and young adults. But I recognized her instantly for what she stood for—the very thing so many of my peers were striving to become.

She swept a passing glance around the room, her eyes sharpening as they passed over her daughter, and I had the distinct feeling like we were all being thoroughly assessed—Reza especially—though I had no idea what for.

"As the protector in charge of the academy portion of this branch," she said, her voice echoing loudly throughout the vaulted room, "I have enlisted the support of Seamus and Cyrus to reach out to their teams this afternoon. As I've known most of you for almost your entire lives," her penetrating blue eyes flashed briefly to me before continuing, "I've taken the opportunity to match you up with the team I think you'd currently fit best with and learn the most from. Our goal is to seamlessly fold you into whichever team you might inevitably join, though changes can and surely will be made before things are finalized. Practical experience is the best way to learn and by acting as passive team members now, we hope that you will more easily transition into active participants in a fraction of the time."

Seamus cleared his throat quietly and opened his mouth like he was going to interrupt. Brave man. I wasn't one who was easily intimidated, but Alleva radiated girl boss energy.

"And," Alleva added with a sigh and discreet eye roll, like she was tolerating a younger brother, "Seamus and Cyrus are of course welcome to make any tweaks they see fit, as Seamus, at least, knows the team chemistry the best. It will be a group effort."

I caught Ro's eye, his brows were furrowed as he studied Alleva. When I looked over at Izzy to see if she knew about this, she shrugged. And judging from the hard line of Atlas's jaw, everyone in the room was unaware of this new strategy. Why were supernatural creatures suddenly flocking to the human realm in droves? And why were attacks so high? Judging by the fact that I'd been attacked by a vampire and a werewolf in less than one month's time, I guess I shouldn't be surprised by the fact there was an increase. While rushing students through to field work didn't sound like the safest approach, I was all for getting more hands-on experience. We could fight each other all day, every day here, but that didn't compare to working with a team against supernatural creatures in the field.

"Has anything like this ever happened before?" I quietly asked Izzy as Alleva, Seamus, and Cyrus started making the rounds through individual students. I tried to ignore my nerves and the way that my stomach tightened at the idea of more or less graduating early. There was excitement lacing those nerves too though—my whole life I'd looked forward to fighting off monsters and protecting humans. Now, it looked like I would finally be given the opportunity.

She shook her head, her normally pixie-like features harder and more tense than usual. "Never. I knew that things were worse than usual, but they must really be bad if they are rushing training like this. Seamus has always been pushing for academy training to get extended by a year or two." Her grey eyes followed him as he walked from student to student. "For him to be on board with this—well, that's not a great sign."

"Are they going to split us all up, you think?" Ro asked, his tone apathetic, but I could tell by the way he tugged on the hem of his shirt that he was legitimately anxious about it.

I rolled my eyes and shoved his shoulder lightly. "Don't worry, big brother, I'll be fine if I don't have you hounding me at all hours of the day. Somehow I'll survive." Still, while I said that, I really *really* hoped that I'd end up with the same team as Ro or Izzy. "Besides, even if we're split up, it's not like we'll be spending all hours of the day with a pro team. I'm sure they have a ton of stuff to do, and it's not like they're all on missions at all times, you know?"

Team Ten hadn't been on another mission since the one Ro joined, and Team Six seemed to be hunkered down for a good while, especially after their last encounter didn't go as planned. Wade was still in the hospital and we hadn't heard any news either way about his recovery. I pushed the concern from my mind—I'd been doing really well at keeping the image of his body lying prone on the hospital bed at bay. He'd be okay. My brain refused to process the chance that he wouldn't. For now, I just figured that no news was good news. And that would have to be enough.

For now.

"Yeah," Izzy said, her lip quirking up on the left, "We'll probably just be with the teams part time and then resume our regular scheduled programming for everything but missions. It doesn't sound like it's a permanent arrangement or anything, just a chance to test drive some teams and see how well we vibe."

I hoped she was right. And even more, I hoped that I was placed with at least one familiar face. Outside of Ten and Six, I hadn't really met any of the other teams—they all seemed to constantly be filtering through the campus on various assignments. Almost none of them had any interaction with students, as far as I could tell.

As they so often did, my eyes landed momentarily on Atlas. The exhaustion I'd noticed just a few moments earlier now seemed replaced by a stiff tension. He and Eli were locked in a stare and I half wondered if they'd found a magic way to talk to each other silently. Neither of them seemed particularly excited by the idea of a new member joining their team, even if it was just temporary.

Would the other teams on campus be as serious and intimidating as Atlas and his group were? Or would they be more inviting, like Ten?

"Rowan Bentley," a curt, clipped voice said. I looked up and found Headmistress Alleva studying the three of us under her cool gaze. She was wearing heels, which seemed like an impractical choice for a protector, and looked kind of absurd amongst all of the sweat and equipment of the gym. But mostly, I was just impressed that her approach had been so silent in those shoes, as she wove her away around the various blue mats. For some reason, that, more than anything, seemed to speak to her stealth. Her silence in stilettos gave off some real assassin vibes.

"Er, yes, that's me," Ro said. His Adam's apple bobbed up and down while she studied him for a long, tense moment.

Seamus and Cyrus were positioned on either side of her, like silent sentinels, clearly letting her take the lead on this. I tried to see Ro through her eyes, fresh and new. Particularly since she seemed to know Cyrus, to have some sort of history with him, I wondered what she knew about us. Cyrus wasn't the type to carry around wallet-sized photos of his kids, showing them off to unsuspecting strangers.

"Right," she said, her eyes tightening ever so slightly. It wasn't like she found him lacking, more so that she didn't quite know what to make him of yet, like an unexpected intruder of sorts. "We're putting you and Isadora with Alpha Ten," she said, jotting something down on a sheet of paper before handing a copy to each of them. "I heard you did well on your first mission with the team, and hopefully they will remain a good fit for you." She cleared her throat for a moment. "Welcome to The Guild. I look forward to seeing what skills and strengths you will bring to our organization. I'm told you are a rather gifted fighter."

Ro grinned slightly at her, but it wasn't filled with warmth and stopped far before it reached his eyes. It seemed that Ro was as hesitant about trusting Alleva as she was about trusting him.

Still, as if in unison, both he and Izzy let out a pair of quiet exhales, no doubt pleased to get placed with our friends. I tried to push the jealousy threatening to bubble up back down. I wanted to join them, badly. And I had a feeling that since she hadn't included me in her address, I wouldn't be. At the very least, I was happy that they were together and with our favorite team.

"What about Max, though," Ro said, while Izzy elbowed him lightly in his side. "Er, mam. Sorry, it's just we prefer to stay together. We've been training together our whole lives and I'm confident that we are more of an asset to this...organization...together than we are apart."

Izzy nodded meekly, and my cheeks warmed. When I looked back over to Alleva to see if she'd agree, I found her studying me with curiosity and narrowed eyes. Where there was a careful acceptance of Ro into the fold, she seemed less sure about me. I tried not to sink too much, knowing that she'd likely heard about the attacks outside of Vanish and maybe, to some extent, even about my not-quite-authorized trips to the research labs. Not exactly a great first impression for my future boss.

I just hoped that at the very least, Reza hadn't spent too much time complaining about me to her mother, otherwise I was screwed.

"Yes, Maxine Bentley," she let out a low exhale, her eyes scanning me from head-to-toe. "Let's put you with Alpha Eight. From what I've heard, it sounds like you've had some exposure recently, so it would probably be best to get you with a decent protective detail, one with discipline." Something about the way she said that ate at me, as if I'd asked to be attacked, or been somehow at fault. "Alpha Eight is quite advanced. I'm sure it'll be a good fit. They are one of our best and I'm sure you could learn a lot from them."

Out of the corner of my eye, I saw Cyrus elbow Seamus roughly in the stomach, causing him to grunt. He coughed quickly, in an attempt to cover up his surprise.

Seamus stepped forward. "Actually, Alleva, I think it would be a better fit to stick Max with Alpha Six. They've been working with her pretty extensively already and it seems to be going well."

My stomach lurched, both excited to be with people I'd at least met, but nervous knowing how temperamental Atlas and his crew were. Their constant mood swings were giving me emotional whiplash. I wasn't exactly sure what Seamus meant by it 'going well,' since I'd only really trained with Atlas for a few days and only had one tutoring session with Wade. If he was going by experience, I had the most with Ten, since they'd taken over the majority of my training.

Alleva whipped her head towards Cyrus before landing her stern expression on Seamus. There was a sharpness to the look, like she was surprised Seamus had challenged her, despite her encouraging him to do so during her entrance speech. "That won't work, I have Reza slotted with them. And while they are processing what happened to cause Wade's traumas, I think it best to keep their apprentice load to one."

I caught sight of Reza out of the corner of my eye, just a few feet away. As usual, her expression was smug and I could tell that she was pleased to be placed with Six. It was no secret that she had her sights on Atlas, both in terms of professional and personal advancement. I studied her rigid posture and then looked back at Headmistress Alleva. I could see the resemblance in their confidence and poise. At first glance, I hadn't noticed all of the similarities between the two women, but now the resemblance was impossible to ignore. Reza looked like Alleva's younger twin.

Seamus straightened, matching Alleva's harsh stare. "Yes, well, as I said, Max has already worked quite a bit with Alpha Six since her arrival, and I think they would be a good fit for her. I've already put them in charge of catching her up with her studies, so it's the natural choice."

My skin prickled slightly, and I turned to see Atlas standing rigid halfway across the room. He was looking through some paperwork, but the absolute stillness of his posture, and the way he'd slightly angled his head had me convinced he was acutely aware of every word in this conversation. I glanced around the rest of the auditorium, finding everyone silent but looking everywhere except in the direction of our little group. Looked like everyone was trying to discreetly eavesdrop. I had a feeling that Headmistress Alleva was challenged, well, never.

I wasn't sure how the power hierarchies really worked at The

Guild, but it was clear that Seamus and Alleva were both top dogs, used to getting their own ways.

"Yes, but Reza will likely be joining their team permanently as soon as she graduates," Alleva responded, tone clipped. She glanced briefly at me, and I had the distinct feeling she didn't think I'd be graduating and joining a team permanently...ever. Did she think that Ro and I were temporary transplants here?

Did I?

In the rush of moving to The Guild, I hadn't really thought about what my goals were long term anymore. But one thing was certain, for as long as Ro and Cyrus were here, I would be as well.

Still, at the thought of Reza so naturally fitting in with the members of Six, my stomach dropped, though I wasn't sure why. I knew that Atlas and Reza were a thing, and Reza was a great fighter. Plus she was the Headmistress's daughter. Bloodlines seemed important to protector culture, no matter how irrelevant they were to me. So in a lot of ways, it made sense she'd join them.

And I wanted to join Ten with Izzy and Ro. Over the last two weeks, I had enjoyed getting to know them all, even Jer, when he toned down the flirtiness. But something about the thought of Reza with Atlas's team had my blood boiling. Maybe after eighteen years of living in isolation, I was secretly drawn in by the drama of Six's hot and cold demeanor. Atlas could be an asshole, but he was never boring.

"Perhaps Reza will join them, eventually" Seamus said, squaring his shoulders and shaking me out of my whirlwind of thoughts. "But those decisions won't officially be made until the end of this year. Shadowing another team might in fact reveal that Reza fits better elsewhere. And, if not, that's also good information for us to know. Every student needs to think of this as a learning experience."

"So where exactly do you suggest slotting my daughter then,"

She arched one perfectly-manicured eyebrow, her voice icey and filled with challenge.

"Alpha Eight should do," Cyrus said, speaking up for the first time. He wasn't looking at Alleva, staring instead at the space between me and Ro. Surprisingly, his expression was rather blank, disinterested almost. It made me think he was deliberately disguising his thoughts and reactions. "I've heard they are quite advanced, one of the best," he added, echoing her earlier words.

Alleva didn't react, beyond her nostrils flaring just slightly. Interestingly, she wasn't looking at Cyrus either. It was like they were deliberately trying to pretend the other wasn't there and I wondered if Alleva was part of the reason Ro and I hadn't been invited to The Guild earlier. Did Alleva want Cyrus here? Or even know that Seamus had called for him?

"Very well," Alleva said, "Maxine Bentley will be working with Alpha Six." She handed me a stack of papers, studying me as her eyes filled with a hard resolve. And then, without another word to me, she turned towards the next group, spine stiff as she walked away.

"What?" Reza yelled, her voice filled with indignation and undisguised fury. She stepped forward, long hair whipping behind her as she cut Alleva off before she reached her next destination. "Mother, you can't be serious. Why does—"

"Enough," Alleva said. The word was uttered so quietly I almost didn't hear it, but Reza snapped her mouth closed as if she'd been slapped.

"Yes, mother. I apologize." Reza slumped slightly, her pale cheeks coloring softly. She looked so defeated that I actually felt bad for her. Alleva's clipped exchange with her daughter made Cyrus seem downright affectionate in comparison.

With a nod, Alleva carried on, Seamus and Cyrus following close behind as they made their way through the rest of the students. Reza levelled a dark glare in my direction, a silent promise in her ice-blue eyes, before she turned back to her friends.

"Great," I muttered, thumbing through the packet of information about my new team. While I was thankful that I wasn't going to be placed with total strangers, I had a nagging feeling that I'd just made two enemies where I'd previously only had one. And that said nothing about the chilly way Atlas was staring at me now. It was pretty damn clear that he was as excited as Reza was about the new arrangement.

This was going to be fun.

6

MAX

When Ro and I arrived back at our suite that night, Cyrus was waiting for us. I was torn between wanting a truce and wanting to yell at him some more about Ralph's treatment in the dungeon. I'd grown up with only two people in my life, so it felt wrong to be harvesting so much frustration and anger towards one of them now. I was terrible at holding a grudge.

"You'll be moving this evening," he said. There was a wall built up in his expression, making his thoughts inaccessible to us. Cyrus wasn't really ever an easy person to read, but he was keeping something from us. And until he decided to let us in on the surprise, it was looking more and more like that invisible little division that he had erected between us would be carved deeper and deeper.

I let out a loud sigh, as my mouth pulled into a frown. What was going on with him? And why was he so dedicated to keeping us out of the loop all of a sudden? In the short time we'd been here, he'd drawn more and more into himself.

I turned to him, making eye contact for the first time since we walked in. There was weariness there, and I clocked the bags taking shape beneath his eyes. Was he sleeping? What wasn't he telling us? My chest warmed at the thought of what he must be going through and I vowed to myself that I'd go easier on him. If he was keeping secrets, it was probably for a good reason; if he wanted some space from us, he'd certainly earned it after years locked up with two teenagers.

"Moving?" Ro asked, tossing his gym bag onto the couch. I studied our living area through Cyrus's eyes. We hadn't really focused much on tidying up recently and I blushed at the pile of dishes in the sink and the random socks tossed around the room. Ro wasn't exactly known for being organized.

"As part of your apprenticeship with the teams, you'll be moving into their cabins. That way you can get a feel for how protectors live their day-to-day lives. It will be a valuable experience for you both." He cleared his throat, glancing briefly at me before returning his attention to Ro. "Seamus and I think that it's the best way to integrate you and throw you into the work headfirst."

"But," I said, my words slow as I processed what he'd just said, what that would mean for me, "we literally just moved in here a couple of weeks ago. Do we really have to stay with them?"

The idea of living with Atlas and his team members had my stomach doing all sorts of flip flops. Rather than question what that meant, I decided to focus more on the fact that I wouldn't be living with Ro anymore—a sentiment that had me equally as uncomfortable, if for other reasons.

"Max isn't on my team though," Ro added, stepping closer to me in a protective gesture. "I don't get why you and Seamus didn't put her with Ten. We both know that we're better together, and no one is going to fight to protect her more than I would."

An odd look passed between Ro and Cyrus, and I had the distinct feeling that I was missing out on some silent conversation they were having.

"I don't need to be babysat, Ro," I said, rolling my eyes,

"though I appreciate the sentiment." A beat of awkward silence passed between the three of us as I moved about the room, picking up some of the random things we'd thrown around throughout the week. "And while I don't need to be babysat, I do think I should be with Ten, Cy. I should be with Ro."

Cyrus's lip twitched into a brief frown, and he met my eyes like he wanted to say something but then he tightened his jaw and didn't speak for several tense, long seconds. "You'll both be where you were assigned, it's final." He took a few steps to our door. "And clean this place up. It looks like animals have been living here. I'll see you downstairs to be taken to your cabins in two hours."

The swiftness with which he reached the decision felt oddly reminiscent of his decision to move us in the middle of the night to The Guild in the first place. Cyrus clearly wasn't one for planning or subtlety. Maybe eventually, I'd grow used to the idea of being shuffled around like a child.

Ro and I sat in silence for an hour and a half, tuning in and out of an old episode of Supernatural. There was something oddly comforting about a show about demon hunters, and Ro and I used to joke that we would one day be a less toxic version of Sam and Dean—hunting monsters together. I think the fact that for the foreseeable future we wouldn't be was settling on us like a heavy fog. Ten minutes before we were supposed to meet Cyrus, we threw our belongings into some bags and did a quick clean of the apartment. I was convinced that procrastination had a way of lighting a fire under my ass, and so I liked to rely on those superpowers as often as I could get away with it. Ten minutes for a pack and house clean? That was some record setting shit right there.

Then again, it also helped that compared to most people our ages, we didn't have a ton of stuff to our names. I'd practically doubled my wardrobe in one shopping session with Izzy.

Briefly, my thoughts wandered back to the cabin, and the giant bookshelf that had been my prized possession. We couldn't bring more than a handful of books with us, but I'd sworn to myself that I'd go back for them all eventually. Until then, I liked the idea of some of our things still remaining at the cabin; it made it easier to leave, knowing that we'd eventually have to come back.

Cyrus led us outside our dorms in silence, and it felt oddly like we were embarking on a completely new, different chapter. My eyes narrowed as I studied him, his limp more pronounced than I'd seen it in a long time. Had he been fighting? I wasn't entirely clear on what his role here was, other than that he was helping Seamus with the teams—was he also going out on missions? He'd been out for days at a time, not checking in with either of us. A fierce wave of protectiveness washed over me and I vowed to spend more time spying on him. For his own safety, of course.

I'd learned quickly that this world was absurdly dangerous, and if the hell realm thought that it was going to take either Cyrus or Ro from me, it had another thing coming.

"Rowan, this is you." Cyrus stopped outside of a large house. It didn't look much like a cabin, but more like a mini mansion. This place was easily three times the size of our place back home, with sprawling green vines climbing up the side and over the roof. There was something so quaint and almost fairytale-like about it.

"This is just for Team Ten?" I studied the area, impressed. The paneling was made of a dark wood, and there was what looked like a trail and fighting ring out back. And while we were a half mile or so away from the main Guild buildings, the area felt private and—homey. My stomach squeezed at the thought that Ro and Izzy would get to play house here. Hopefully they would be up for having me as a visitor during all of my free time.

Arnell opened the door before Cyrus had a chance to knock, a bright grin splitting his face.

Arnell had one of those smiles that made it impossible to not reciprocate. It lit up his whole expression, extending a warm glow to his eyes.

"Awesome! You're here," he said, glancing shyly at Ro after nodding once to me and Cy.

Ro cleared his throat and nodded awkwardly, and I reminded myself to ask him again about what was going on between them. Whatever it was, they'd have to get over it if they were going to be quite literally shacking up together. Plus, I was all for Team Arnell when it came to Ro's future happiness. I didn't know him well, but it took just one single introduction to solidify that Arnell was a good person in my mind.

"Cool, well, come on in." Arnell looked over at me again and scrunched up his nose. "Sorry you don't get to join us yet, Max, but hopefully soon." He turned to Cyrus. "Thanks sir, we'll take it from here, have a good night."

Ro grabbed my hand and squeezed without looking at me. Then he walked through the door, and my stomach sank. I felt like I was being a big baby, but when you went your whole life with only one absolute constant, changing it sucked and was hard.

Cyrus turned and walked further away from the campus. We walked in silence for a few minutes, the awkwardness of our new dynamic settling over me in uncomfortable waves. "Don't worry, Max. I know this is going to be difficult for you both, it's not easy for me either as much as I'd like to pretend otherwise. But you'll be happy to know that Team Six is literally right next door, so it's not like Ro is moving across the state."

A slow grin crept across my face at this small concession. And we continued our trek in a much more companionable silence until we came up to an identical building to the one that had just swallowed up Ro and his suitcase of belongings.

Unlike Ten, however, Six didn't give me a warm welcome home introduction.

Cyrus knocked and after a few minutes and what sounded like bickering, Eli swung open the door. He glanced briefly in my

FORGING THE GUILD

direction before looking back at Cyrus. "Thanks Uncle Cyrus, we'll take it from here. She's in good hands."

With that dismissal, Cyrus nodded and turned to me like he wanted to say something. Instead, he swallowed the thought down, and turned to go to wherever his home was on this campus, while I followed Eli in and shut the door behind me.

I don't know why, but I was sort of expecting it to smell like a locker room in here. Something about three dudes living together just didn't scream clean and sparkly. But this place was spotless and absolutely stunning.

We walked into a large, rustic living room, with a huge TV and what looked like every video game console ever made. Deep, black leather couches framed the space—they were the kind of couches you could sink into and gladly be eaten up by. Perfect reading and Netflix-watching couches. I was practically swooning at the thought. Protectors certainly seemed to have unlimited sources of funds and I wondered again why Cy would give all of this up to live in our tiny tent of a house back home.

The living room opened up into a large kitchen with all new, stainless steel appliances and a large wooden island that looked to double as a bar. Everything was tidy and had its own place. It was like Marie Kondo had designed the setup for them and I found myself smiling at the idea of Eli in an apron cooking up a well-balanced meal for the boys and Declan when they were too lazy to walk to the cafeteria. This kitchen certainly explained why I didn't see them there for every meal.

"Here, I'll grab your bags," Eli said, taking them from me awkwardly. He was avoiding eye contact and I got the impression he was extremely uncomfortable with having me here. His dark wavy hair was slightly wet and curling more than usual, like he'd just taken a shower. Instead of his usual workout gear, he was dressed in dark jeans and an olive-green sweater. I got a subtle waft of cologne and I half wondered if he was getting ready for a date later tonight.

I hadn't seen the store clerk Eileen since walking in on her and Eli...erm...engaging in adult activities. And the thought of him seeing her again left a hollow, anxious hole in my stomach. How many girls would I have to worry about walking in on while living here? If need be, I could just keep to my room during visiting hours.

A door upstairs slammed shut, so someone else was here, just not part of the welcoming committee. I tried not to let it grate against my nerves, but it was weird to not feel welcome in the space where you were supposed to indefinitely be living. I felt like an unwanted intruder. Probably because I was. No one here had asked that I join their team, even if it was only temporary.

"I, uh, set up a room for you," he said, leading me up the stairs and down a long hallway. We had one empty room. I hope you like yellow."

"I can live with yellow," I said. We walked past three shut doors, one of which had some loud rock music playing. It wasn't a song I'd ever heard before. "Who's the owner of the stereo?"

Eli scratched the back of his neck before opening the second-last door on the left. "Dec."

Moody, angsty music? Yeah, I guess that was on brand for Declan. She'd been ignoring me, like Eli and Atlas, since their return from the mission. Before they left, I thought Declan and I had started to bond. She'd even hung out and watched movies with Izzy, Ro, and me. And while she didn't seem completely comfortable in our company, I'd thought there was potential for friendship to grow eventually, albeit slowly. But now, things just seemed so different—closed off between us somehow.

"Where's Atlas?" I asked, trying to shake off the tension rolling through my body.

"He was in a meeting with Alleva and probably went to sit with Wade for a bit." Eli exhaled softly. "He's been spending most of his free time there since the mission."

The Alleva bit surprised me, but I welcomed the opportunity to ask about Wade. "How is he?"

Eli leaned against the door frame and let out a low sigh. He studied me, his warm, amber eyes so unreadable, like his thoughts and emotions were completely cut off from me. I watched as a single droplet of water fell from a curl down his face. He wiped it away absentmindedly. "Honestly?"

"Always," I said.

At my answer, a sad, almost imperceptible grin pulled at his lips. "We don't know. He hasn't woken up yet and we're not really sure why."

"Was it a vampire attack?" I asked, pressing a finger against where I'd been bitten. It was becoming an unconscious habit. "Or werewolf?" There were other beasts of course, but those were the two The Guild seemed to focus on the most and the two most commonly spotted outside of the hell realm. They were also the most aggressive species when it came to attacks on humans. Probably why they held such real estate in human folklore. The myths emerged from half truths.

"Both. We don't really know, none of us were there during the attack." He swiped some hair off his forehead before rubbing the back of his neck. He seemed more fidgety than usual.

I shook my head, shocked. "Vampires and wolves were working together? Is that a thing?"

"No, it's not. And forget I mentioned it, it's not really something for students to be concerned with right now." He shook his head, and I had a feeling that was all I was going to get out of him about the issue, because in the same breath, he turned and pushed into the room.

I peeked around the corner and grinned. The room was beautiful. Dark gray curtains framed a window that ran almost the full length of the room. It faced the woods, so I'd have lots of privacy which was nice. A huge king-size bed sat in the middle of the room, looking like a cloud with all of the pillows set up in perfect rows. My eyes were instantly drawn to a bookshelf. It was packed with novels and DVDs, which apparently were still a thing, and a small record collection.

"This room is amazing," I said, plopping down on the bed. It was even more comfortable than it looked—the perfect mix of firm and soft. "It's really mine? For now, I mean?"

A shadow of a grin lifted his lips as he nodded.

"Who gets credit for decorating?" I couldn't imagine any of the guys or Declan choosing yellow for a spare room, or organizing it so perfectly with accent details throughout.

A dark look crossed Eli's face and he cleared his throat. "It belonged to someone else. We had a fifth on our team. Declan's cousin, Sarah."

The word lingered in the air like frost. Had.

"I'm sorry," I said, meaning it. "When did she die?"

"About six months ago." He sat down next to me and smiled softly, his expression lost in a memory as he looked over at me. "You would've liked her. She was hilarious and almost nonsensically brave. A real fucking force. Kind of like Declan in that way. Although she was American, so she didn't have Dec's awesome accent."

I reached over and squeezed his hand. I'd never lost anyone before. But so much as the thought of losing Ro or Cyrus, or even Izzy cut me to the core. Suddenly Declan's distance, her guarded distrust made so much more sense. She was the loner of the group, that much had been obvious. But how much of it was because of her grief?

"Were Declan and Sarah close?" I lowered my voice, like I was trying to protect the fragile conversation. There was a vulnerability in Eli's eyes that I hadn't seen before.

"Like sisters. She doesn't like to talk about her much anymore."

I looked around at the room again, at all of the possessions lining the shelves. Suddenly it felt like a museum, an altar to a girl they'd all lost. It had been six months and no one had put away her things, or used the room. "Are you sure it's okay that I stay here?"

He shrugged, his lips pulled down in the corner. "No other options. I'm sure it'll be hard, for Dec especially, but she knows that you need a place to sleep. It's time that we cleared out the cobwebs of the room and got to healing more fully." Eli's face flushed as he looked down at our grasped hands. I think we'd both forgotten we were touching. As if burned, he pulled his hand away and cleared his throat. "But—uh—look, I wouldn't mention her much. She was in the process of bonding to Wade and Atlas, so everyone is still pretty raw."

I nodded, staring at the pale-yellow wall in front of us. "Right, totally. I won't, I promise." I felt weird sitting here suddenly, like I was sitting in the room of a ghost.

"Are, are you sure it's okay, me staying here? I can take a different room, if you guys want to, you know, preserve this one or whatever. I can even take the couch if you want."

Eli pushed himself off the bed and moved towards the door. "Nah, like I said, it's cool. Honestly, I think it's good to breathe new life into the room. It wigs me out, having it here unused. You can redecorate or whatever, if you want. I don't know how long you'll be here, but while you are, consider it and everything in it, yours." And with that, he left, closing the door behind him.

Cool. So now I was moved in with a team that didn't seem to really want me here, living in a dead girl's room. A dead girl they all loved and were clearly still mourning. It wasn't exactly a good way to inspire comradery or get on their good side.

I unzipped my suitcase, pulling out some pajamas to sleep in. I couldn't bring myself to put my things away in the dresser or closet.

Suddenly, the absolute silence of the room unsettled my nerves, my chest tightening. Eli's story about Sarah just served to iron in the realities of being a protector—and all the grief that came with it. For a brief second, I desperately wanted to run downstairs and see Ro. I'd have to settle with texting—it would be the first step towards severing my codependency.

And for the silence? I swept my fingers along the edge of records, pulling one out at random. Cy didn't have much tolerance for music, so I didn't grow up with much until I discovered

Spotify. Even then, outside of various soundtracks, even I knew that my tastes were underdeveloped. After a minute of fidgeting with the record player, I figured it out, and listened as a slow, eerie, and almost sad song swept through the room, the sound somehow both crisp and smooth.

As I sat back against the pillows, I allowed myself to linger on the fact that Wade and Atlas had been bonded before. I tried to think about Atlas being warm to anyone. The protective edge was easy enough to imagine, but I wondered if he and Sarah had ever been something more.

And now, with Reza in the picture, I wondered how he really felt about The Guild slowly pushing him to bond again. It was clear from earlier today that Alleva had a very specific future in mind for him and her daughter.

My stomach tightened at the thought of Reza sleeping in this room. Would Wade be forced to bond with her too? Eli?

A sharp pressure in my jaw grounded me and I forced myself to relax the muscles in my face, to relax my hands that were suddenly balled into fists. I didn't need to fit in with Six forever. Right now, I just needed to get through the night, and then I could sort through all of the new emotions whirling through my body like an unwelcome swarm of bees.

I took a deep breath in, letting the music roll over me.

7

ELI

I spent most of the night after Max's arrival staring at my ceiling, listening to the records she was playing on the other side of my wall. I was never interested in Sarah. Hell, I'd practically grown up with her so she was sort of like a little sister. But now, I was acutely aware of the fact that there was a girl I was annoyingly interested in dancing around a few feet away from my bed. Her movements sounded chaotic and clunky, and it was clear she didn't know the words to any of the songs that she played. There were several times I bit the inside of my cheeks to prevent the loud laugh from escaping.

My door smashed open, and I sat up, annoyed by the intrusion. Atlas walked into my room, throwing not-so-covert glances at the room Max now occupied, as if he could see her through the wall like fucking Superman. He wasn't one for encroaching on privacy, so seeing him in my room without knocking threw me for a bit of a whirlwind.

What had his panties in a bunch?

"She's here, then?" he asked. He scratched the stubble on his chin, and I grinned at his obvious discomfort.

Ah, there it was, that subtle muscle tick in his brow. Guess it wasn't so much of a 'what' as a 'who' then. Getting stuck with someone new threw us all for a loop and we were all caught off guard. But when we learned that the person we'd be mentoring was Max...well, we were all a bit thrown. Especially since we'd recently agreed on keeping a careful, objective distance from her while we looked out for any future monsters she was likely to attract.

Alleva threw a wrench into that plan. And a colossal fucking wrench at that.

"She's here. Been in her room all night though. I think she's a bit afraid of us?" Afraid maybe wasn't the right word. It was glaringly obvious however that she wasn't comfortable around any of us. And honestly, that was totally fair. We'd been pretty hot and cold with her; I had anyway, Atlas was mostly just a consistent dickhead.

Did she feel the same pull that we did? Did Cyrus teach her about bonds at all? I doubted it. From what my father said, it seemed like Cyrus was, until recently, determined to live his life as a hermit exile, ignoring everything about the hell realm and our calling. What made someone like that suddenly choose to adopt two kids? And then why choose to suddenly come back, bulldozing into the life he'd abandoned so many years ago? It didn't make sense, but my father blew me off any time I voiced the question.

"Good," Atlas said, before plopping down unceremoniously in the chair across from my bed. He was exhausted. I hadn't seen him like this in a while. Too many stressors were taking too much of a toll on him. If we weren't careful, he was going to explode sooner rather than later. And none of us were equipped to handle the hurricane that was Atlas on the edge.

"How's Wade?" I asked, though I knew that nothing had changed in his condition. If it had, Atlas would've been ten shades brighter and significantly more excited. The longer Wade stayed in this weird coma, the more drained Atlas seemed to get.

None of us would voice it out loud, but we all knew that each day that Wade didn't wake up, we were creeping closer to the probability that he wouldn't.

And now, at this point, I was half expecting to wake up one day and for Atlas to be gone. The mere thought of it made my stomachache. This team was my family, my home. And it felt like one-by-one, we were being picked off like we were all playing in a sadistic game of musical chairs. Only with monsters. And bureaucratic bullshit. Atlas was our leader, but Wade was our glue.

He shook his head, confirming my thoughts—no new developments. His eyes drifted towards my wall, and he cocked an eyebrow.

"She—er, found Sarah's record collection," I said, not quite meeting Atlas's eyes. He hadn't set foot in that room since Sarah died. No one had, really. Not until today when I tried to dust it off a bit and make it look hospitable. I cleared my throat and ran my hand through my hair, biting back a grin at the thought of Max on the other side of the wall, dancing to some Amy Winehouse. "What's the play here, Atlas?"

"Play?" He kicked his head back and looked up at the ceiling, like the wood paneling held the answers to the universe. He exhaled softly, using his feet to roll the chair from side to side. "What do you mean?"

"I mean that we all agreed to keep our distance from her." I pointed to the wall in case he needed a reminder of how well that was working out. "Not exactly going to be possible now, is it? So how do you want to handle this?"

Silence. After a few impossibly long seconds, I was almost convinced he'd fallen asleep. He tilted his head forward, like he was trying to see into the next room, his brows pinching together.

All at once, I remembered that Atlas was only a couple years older than me. He didn't have all the answers and the rest of us had a bad habit of expecting him to. It sort of came with the territory of being group leader and generally acting like a boss. But seeing him now, it was alarmingly clear that he was just as lost as I was. Max's arrival had torn up the blueprint for how he navigated our world, restructured our actions and reactions into some weird, unrecognizable new normal.

"I don't know," he said, finally, his head shaking softly like whatever answer he was hoping was written across the wall wasn't. It was just blank instead, empty. A chill ran through my bones. Atlas never sounded so unsure, so broken. "I honestly don't know how we handle any of this right now. We go on missions. We find out what happened to Wade. We get him to wake up. We train her to the best of our ability—" his hand tensed on the arm of the chair "while maintaining our distance." He met my eyes. "I'm losing my grip on it this month, I can't control it like I usually can. I can't suppress it. I don't know why. But her being here, following us around—it's dangerous, Eli."

I frowned, not quite sure what to say. Atlas didn't talk about this much, and we all took his lead when he did. "It's probably the stress, man. With Wade. It's been a chaotic fucking month."

He nodded, but didn't seem convinced. "Still, her being here, it makes things so much more complicated—our plans are fragile right now at best. With her here? I just don't want them to shatter."

For a while after he left, I drifted off between waking and sleep, listening to the soft lull of the music next door. For a brief dream-laced moment, I allowed myself to think about the wall separating my bed from Max's disappearing. My mind danced over the possibilities of what it would feel like, my skin on hers. The thought alone was enough to get my dick hard, and I was half convinced that I just needed to get her out of my system already before she completely ruined my focus. Divided attention did not yield good results in our world.

A harsh vibration pulled me out of my fantasy and I looked

down to a text from my father—a major boner killer if ever there was one. It was just past midnight, way beyond his usual bedtime. Seamus was always part of that early to bed, early to rise crowd.

He wanted to meet with me ASAP at my pond, an urgency to the text that had me shuffling my legs through each of my pant legs in record time. It was rare for Seamus to want to meet with me alone, without the guys that is, and rarer still for him to want to meet this late.

I left my room quietly, standing for a moment outside of Max's door. For a hard second, I felt bad leaving on her first night. Which was ridiculous. It wasn't like it mattered if I was here either way, and she wasn't exactly alone. Declan and Atlas were both within shouting distance if some big bad barged into her room to take her away. Shaking off the irrational anxiety, I took the steps two at a time, still managing to escape the house without a sound.

The night air was crisp as I wove around the trees, carving my familiar path to the pond on the edge of Guild territory. I'd made my way there so many times over the years that I could do it blindfolded without tripping over a single root. When the clearing opened up, I saw the moon reflecting down on the water like it was made of nothing but glass. The fresh mossy smell of wet bark filled my nose and I listened to the absolute stillness surrounding me.

Father aside, being here tonight would do wonders for calming the hurricane of sensations brought about by Max. It'd been weeks since I'd come down here at night and I forgot how tranquil it was when no one was around. These moments of peace were rare in our world.

As if on cue, I spotted Seamus pacing back and forth along the opposite edge of the pond, a tightness to his step. His anxiety stuck out like a sore thumb out here, the only disturbance to an otherwise refreshing calm. I jogged over, reaching him quickly, suddenly filled with an extreme need to know what he'd called me out of bed for.

"Dad," I said, my voice low, as if speaking at a normal volume out here would shatter the environment. "Everything okay?" My words were slow, almost as if I were talking to a child and not the man who raised me and taught me to decapitate creatures from hell.

His head snapped to me, and I realized instantly that he was so lost in his thoughts that he hadn't even heard my arrival. With acute protector hearing, that had to mean that whatever maze he was traveling through in his mind was draining almost all of his focus. Seamus Bentley was not the sort of man who ever lost focus.

"Eli," he said, walking up to me in two long strides and clasping my shoulder with his large, calloused hand. "Good, good, you're here. Finally."

I wasn't sure what he meant by that; I ran here as soon as I'd received the text.

Rather than respond, I stood in silence, urging him to continue. It was clear from the intensity pooling in his black eyes that whatever he had to talk about was important.

"I called you here for a few things," he said as if he was giving me a report for an assignment. He dropped the harsh grip on my shoulder and stared out at the pond as if listening to hear if we had any eavesdroppers. "First, I wanted to inform you that Alleva came to me tonight and asked that I consider you as a potential bondmate for Reza. Second—"

"What?" I said, loud enough to scare a few birds from a nearby tree. So much for keeping the peace out here.

"I know how you feel about the girl, and about Alleva, but I promised her we'd consider it. With the attacks so close to campus, she's growing paranoid and fearing for her daughter's safety. It's understandable and I don't entirely blame her. Our women—our strong women especially—seem to so often be targeted by the beasts lately. After Max's experiences these last weeks, that's only been confirmed."

"What about Atlas and Wade?" While neither of them was exactly excited by the prospect of bonding to Reza, their father had all but decided it would come to pass. It was just a matter of when, and both of them were pushing for an exceptionally long wait. Years even. And with what happened to Sarah, there was due reason for the delay. That sort of mourning was a long process for our kind, even if the bond wasn't completely solidified.

He shook his head, his eyes refocusing on me. "They will still be bonded to her as well. But with things as perilous as they are now, Alleva is eager to see her daughter with added protection. And, by her logic, this would solidify the ties to your team even more."

He didn't say what I know we were both thinking; that the ties would be solidified for everyone but Declan. She'd remain on the outskirts and if she wasn't bonded to any of us on the team, she'd likely be moved to another one as soon as the bonds were formed.

"And Declan?"

Seamus's lips dipped, as the exertion of his frantic announcement slipped from his face. "I know that we talked about her bonding with you or with the boys as another option. But Alleva wants three for Reza, so either you take the third spot, or she brings in someone else. And there's no telling who that someone else will be."

Three bondmates wasn't completely unheard of, but I had never personally encountered a female protector with more than two. If Alleva was dead set on this arrangement, it meant things were even worse off than we thought.

"I take it her trip didn't yield the results she was hoping for?" I stared at a small ripple in the pond from either a fish or a frog. My pulse was suddenly racing, and I was almost upset with my father for choosing this spot to have this conversation. It felt wrong to distort the energy around here, to disrupt it.

He shook his head, dropping down on his ass to sit in the grass. I followed suit, not even pretending to care about the dirt like I might under other circumstances. "She's learned that all headquarters are stretched thin. There have been more deaths of our people recorded in the last year than ever before, with attacks getting closer and closer to Guild territory. It's like the creatures are amping up to strike together. No one understands it, no lab has noticed anything remarkable or distinct about the creatures captured from these attacks." He exhaled sharply. "But it's a deeply skewed battle, son. And we are on the losing end."

My father wasn't the type to raise alarms without evidence, so I had no doubt that he earnestly believed every word he was saying, every fear he was disclosing. "And do you—do you think that I should bond with Reza?"

I held my breath hoping he'd say no, that the offer was absurd, and that Declan or Max was the way to go, if I was required to bond at all. His silence was my only answer, and it was clear as crystal.

"What about Max?" I said, unable to hold the question in. He'd mentioned her to me once or twice over the years. He hadn't met her until I did, of course, but he often spoke of his brother's adopted ward and hinted more than once since their arrival that she might be a good match for me, a good addition to our team. When he encouraged her to move in instead of Reza, I had assumed that same logic still applied. Now, well, now I wasn't so sure.

I had never really given bonding too much thought, realizing it was nothing more than a requirement, a helpful tool for doing our work. Hell, I'd even been excited by the idea of bonding to Declan eventually, to tighten our synchronicity during missions. But now with this news, I felt my stomach sink—every thought somehow ghosting around the idea of being bonded to Max. When had she sunk so deeply into my consciousness? Why did the idea of her being bonded to someone else set my skin on fire?

"Max is not an option," he said, eventually halting the thoughts skating through my mind like a whirlwind. "I spoke with Cyrus tonight, after my meaning with Alleva. He doesn't want her to bond."

"Like, ever?" I asked, stunned. What I didn't add was the fear that he just didn't want her to bond with me, that he found me lacking as a life match for her.

"Like ever," he echoed, his eyes baring down on me, like he was searching for something in my own, trying to decipher whatever emotions were playing out across my features. "And the thing is, Eli, that the way he talks about her—it's with such impermanence. I don't know how long he plans to stay here with them, but I know that it isn't forever. I know my brother well, and he has one foot out the door, like he's simply waiting for an excuse or a reason to grab them both and disappear again."

In a flash, I saw it in his black stare—the pain that I saw in the rare moments his guard was down. He didn't cover it up this time, let me see as it took over his expression. It was a warning.

"You think that even if she bonded, she wouldn't stick around," I said, the words piercing through the air as my throat blocked up at the thought. It was the very thing that my mother had done to him when I was young.

My father loved her in a way that she didn't or couldn't reciprocate and, eventually, she left us both. It was one of the most taboo things a protector could do—willingly break a bond. When it was done, it created a fracture, a piece of each person was forever destroyed, completely incapable of regrowing. Rather than risk the pain again, Seamus chose to never join another bond, never so much as enter into any intimate relationship.

And when I turned to him again, I saw the truth as plain as day. He'd rather see me in a political bond with Reza than have me experience that kind of torment, that kind of soul-ripping abandonment. I nodded, not knowing what else to say. I understood where he was coming from, even if I didn't completely agree, not yet.

"That brings me to the second thing I wanted to discuss with you," he said, resting his hand on my knee and squeezing gently. He wasn't one for overt affection, but I knew that he loved me and wanted to provide comfort when he could. Sometimes the thought alone was enough. "There's something Cy is keeping from me. Something to do with the girl. I know some of the circumstances of how she came to live with him, but there's more there that he hasn't shared. I can feel it."

"What do you mean?" I asked, curiosity engulfing whatever lingering pain the mention of my mother had dredged up.

"He's so attached to the girl, so protective of her. He's hiding something from me. And the way that he feels towards her. It's just so unlike him. He's so sentimental."

He knew Cyrus better than I did, but I didn't think anybody would use the word sentimental to describe him.

"Do you think she's really his?" The thought of being potentially related to Max caused a ripple of revulsion to roll through my stomach. Had I felt so strongly about a cousin?

As if sensing my discomfort, he let out a quiet chuckle, breaking the tension. "Don't worry, son. I'm certain she's not, but there's something about where she came from that he's keeping to himself. I—"

I narrowed my eyes at him as he tried to find whatever words he was searching for.

"I want you to get a blood or a hair sample if you can. Discreetly. Discuss it with no one but me. And I want you to keep her close. I asked before that you and your team watch out for her, that you protect her. But now I want you to observe her as well. Learn what you can and report back to me what you find out. If I'm going to risk my family, and my position trying to help this girl, I want to know what exactly we are taking these risks for. Can—can you do that for me, please?"

My thoughts whirled with everything he'd thrown at me, a heavy ball of iron settling in my stomach. Without another word, I nodded.

And when I returned home, I stared at the wall separating me from Max, wishing with every fiber of my being that she was just a normal girl, not some mystery protector shrouded in temptation and impenetrable secrecy.

8
MAX

I woke up with a tattered novel pressed between my face and one of the pillows on my bed. I had slept like a rock, which was surprising. I was low-key pretty proud of myself though—first time in a place without Ro or Cyrus, and I survived. Had to count for something, right?

Pushing through a yawn, I grabbed one of my bags, tossing my clothes around until I located my toothbrush and toiletries. Usually all I wanted in the mornings was a nice long run, but it was a Saturday and I decided that I had earned the day off.

I collected a large towel from the bottom of my bag and opened my door, trying to be as quiet as possible. I felt like a stranger here, like I was snooping around in someone else's house. And I guess I kind of was. Living here—my time with Six—was temporary.

Eli didn't really show me where the bathroom was. I had a half bath next door to my room, but I needed a shower, desperately. And other than Declan's room, I had no idea where any of these doors led.

I shut the door softly and turned left, stopping at the door next to mine. I knocked twice, but didn't hear a response. I felt a little guilty snooping, but the guys weren't exactly the most welcoming bunch, and if I could find the bathroom without any help, that was the option I was going with. While I liked to pretend that I was brave, I was under no delusions in this case. Six was an intimidating bunch and while Eli was welcoming last night, I wasn't exactly sure what my time here would look like.

I pushed the door open, and found myself in a green and black bedroom, but a setup almost identical to mine. I breathed a sigh of relief when I realized the room was empty. While I was tempted to explore, to learn a little bit more about the guys, it felt too invasive. Was this Wade's room? Or Eli's?

For the most part, the space was remarkably well organized, with everything perfectly in place. Well, almost everything. I looked down at the ground and blushed. There was a pair of what looked like haphazardly discarded red panties sticking out from under the bed. Eli's room then, if I had to guess. Something about his flirtatious energy told me that out of everyone in the house, he had the most frequent bedroom guests. I suppressed a shiver, uncomfortable with the thought of him entertaining girls on the other side of my wall. Which was ridiculous. This was his home. And it had been my wall all of two seconds.

Briefly, I thought about the possibility of whether or not the underwear belonged to Eileen, and then my entire body heated at the thought of that night in the club. Images of him pounding into her from behind filled my mind, my stomach clenching at the thought of someone, of him, doing that to me. Did the guys have women over a lot? They definitely wouldn't be allowed to have any humans on campus, but I wondered if I could expect to see Reza popping in and out of Atlas's room throughout the week.

With an involuntary shiver, I left the room and closed the door. Walking immediately across from what I assumed was Eli's room, I knocked. No answer. I took a breath, debating with myself about whether I should open this door or not. Curiosity won out, and I opened the door, letting out a relieved sigh. It looked like an office—probably where they did a bunch of their prep work for missions. Judging by my brief time at The Guild, it was clear that field teams spent a lot of time analyzing old strategies and migration patterns of supernaturals. It wasn't quite as 'fight-kill-celebrate' as shows like Buffy made vampire hunting seem.

I scanned the computer monitors and books piled all over the desks. I stepped into the room, excited by the possibility of going with the guys on their next mission.

Messy scrawl covered discarded notebook pads all over the place—names of places, of people, of various supernatural sightings. Most of it didn't make any sense to me. There was an abandoned mug sitting on one of the surfaces, the lingering scent of stale coffee filtering through the room. My fingers traced the edges of a large leather chair, the seat imprinted slightly with continual use. I thought of Atlas, the constant stern expression of his face, and imagined this seat was his. There was something so careful, so calculating about his every movement, that the thought of him spending most of his spare time in this room seemed clear as day. He wasn't the sort to enter into any situation without complete control. The guy was an ass, but even I could admit that there was plenty for me to learn from him if I could just swallow my pride.

And then there was Sarah. My mind couldn't stop spinning up versions of her all night. Who was she? What was she like? What were Atlas and Wade like when she was around? Was Atlas more...human when he was with her? I saw the way he looked at Wade—stern and serious as always, but with a heavy undertone of legitimate affection. It was the way that Ro often looked at me. Was Atlas capable of shedding his professionalism in small, isolated moments? Did Six ever crowd onto the couch after a long day, watching bad movies, eating greasy food, and laughing uncontrollably—attempting to soothe the pressure and fatigue that came with being protectors?

I turned, ready to leave, when I found what looked like a stack of blueprints. With a quick glance at the door, I listened, making sure nobody was coming. For a moment, I stood still, debating whether or not to look more closely, to see what they were working on. Eventually, my curiosity won out. I'd be joining them on missions soon enough, so the sooner I was up to speed, the better I would be at aiding them. I shuffled through the papers, feeling like a proper James Bond, until I found one with a lazy 'Lab' scrawled in the upper right corner. I studied the piece of paper, and the numbers written along the margins. Were these codes? My heart pounded, racing with the thought of what this was.

I looked down the page, flipping through several more until I was certain I found the spot I recognized—Ralph's jail cell. Committing the piece to memory, I backed away with a shit-eating grin on my face. This was step one if I wanted to break him out. I turned, ready to leave until I saw a folder sitting below one of the monitors. My name was printed in large letters along the label. Unable to resist the temptation, I walked towards that side of the desk and flipped the manila file open. What did they have on me? Cyrus was always so cagey about how he found me. Did The Guild know more?

"Do you frequently go snooping through other people's things?"

Startled, I dropped the file and saw Declan standing in the doorway, a thunderous expression on her face.

"I uh—" I started, searching for an explanation until I realized that Declan was very very wet, and very very naked. Well, almost naked. A white towel was perched precariously low across her chest, the cloth folded casually. So casually, that if she breathed too deeply, I was convinced it would fall to the floor. Her long dark hair was an even deeper shade when wet, and I stared at the way it clung to her neck and chest in long waves.

Her intense green eyes were framed by her dark lashes, the individual strands clumped together and highlighting the color even more than usual. I'd seen beautiful girls before. The Guild was full of them. And I was no stranger to shows and movies with stunning actresses. But somehow they all seemed to pale in comparison to Declan. There was something so otherworldly about her beauty, the way it was filtered with an intense strength and intellect. Everything about her was intimidating and made my skin tingle with an unusual anxiety. Wherever she was in a room, my eyes seemed immediately drawn to her, like a moth to a flame.

I sucked in a breath, the scent of strawberries clinging to the air around her, all but completely erasing the smell of musty paper and coffee from before.

She cleared her throat and I jumped. How long had I been staring?

"S-s-sorry," I said, moving quickly towards the door. Until I realized that she was blocking it and I couldn't get past until she moved. "I was looking for the bathroom."

Declan looked slowly from one side of the office to the other before meeting my eyes. Deep, intimidating green stared back at me. "I know you've lived a sheltered life, Max, but in case you haven't figured it out yet—this is not a bathroom."

I swallowed, absolutely still while Declan watched me. It felt like I was being stalked by a predator, like she could pounce at any second. Sometimes she seemed approachable, almost friendly, but other times, like now, I could all but feel the way her eyes peeled me back, layer by layer.

"I'm sorry. Really. It's just, I've never been in a team's office before and it was hard to turn away. I thought I might be able to familiarize myself with some of the stuff you guys are working on, so that I could be more helpful and jump in where needed." Honesty. Maybe honesty was the way to go here. "And then, I saw a file with my name on it and got curious. I know almost nothing about my history, about where I came from. I don't even know who my birth parents are, and I just thought—"

Understanding crossed her face, the lines of her expression softening just a touch as she leaned against the doorframe. She pulled the wet strands of her hair back into a top bun, and I tried not to watch the way the movement pulled her towel a breath lower. "You thought you might find the answers in there."

I nodded.

"Hate to disappoint you, kid, but the only info in there is what Cyrus and Seamus have told us. And I have a feeling that's even less than what Cy has told you over the years. That, and there's also info recording most of your stats since you've been here." Her eyes moved from my face down to my neck. "And some pictures of your attack." She pushed away from the door and walked into the hallway. I followed, certain that I'd outworn my welcome in the office. She stopped at the next door and pushed it open. "This is the bathroom."

Damn. One door away from finding it on my own. Rotten luck.

She took a long breath and quietly exhaled, her eyes studying my face with renewed focus. "Not knowing where you're from must be really hard. I have a few contacts across different Guild locations, so I can put some feelers out there and let you know if I get any bites. But in the meantime, I'd try to spend more energy focusing on your future, not your past. As impossible as that may seem—" she paused and glanced over to my—to Sarah's —room, though I didn't think the movement was conscious.

"Thank you. I'd really appreciate that." And I meant it, though I doubted I'd be able to outright ignore my desire to know more about my past, about where I came from.

When her eyes landed back on mine, I could feel every ounce of air leaving my lungs. Suddenly, I was excruciatingly aware of how close we were standing, the fibers of her towel whispering against the skin of my arm. Every inhale brought us momentarily closer, and I could feel my skin come alive with a tingling energy. I studied her face with a new awareness, the soft curves of her full lips, the high ridges of her cheekbones. I wasn't exactly sure what feeling was rushing through me. A desire to befriend Declan, to be close to her. But I couldn't decipher or untangle the thoughts beyond that.

Suddenly unable to handle the building tension, I took a step back and glanced around the hallway. I cleared my throat, waiting for my heartrate to drop back down. "And I'm sorry," I said, thinking back to last night. I wasn't the only one with a past. "Eli told me about your cousin. I can't imagine how hard that must have been. To have lost someone so close to you."

Her green eyes glazed over as she took a step back, like she was making room for whatever wall she was building back up between us. While her face was guarded, I knew what lay beneath that wall—Declan was in pain. A piercing, excruciating pain. "Death is a part of this life. What happened to Sarah will happen to all of us who take the field path. We are naive if we think otherwise."

I nodded, suddenly feeling ridiculous for bringing this up. It was clear she wasn't comfortable talking about her cousin, least of all with someone who was practically a stranger. And I couldn't blame her. Ro and Cy were the only family I had. But if I lost them—I wasn't sure how someone could survive that sort of grief. The thought alone was enough to shatter me.

"Still," I said, gripping my towel and toiletries to my chest for comfort, "that doesn't erase the pain. And I just, I want you to know that I appreciate you letting me borrow her room. I promise that I don't take that gift lightly and I will take great care of everything in it while I'm around." With a soft smile and a nod, I walked into the bathroom before quietly closing the door, as if afraid of shattering the moment.

When I heard Declan walk away, I let out a long, impossibly heavy breath and tried to still my racing heartbeat. I couldn't tell if my pulse was racing from being caught snooping, from the conversation, or from the way my eyes seemed to glue themselves to every inch of Declan's skin. Was it guilt or fear or something else entirely? Unwilling to linger too much on my discomfort, I readied for a shower. And, just in case, I'd make it a cold one.

9

MAX

When I returned from my shower, it was to a series of texts from Izzy. Apparently in light of current events and moving in with teams, we no longer had the afternoon off. We were expected to be in the gym within the hour for a meeting with Alleva and some extra training sessions. By the time I pushed my limbs into my workout clothes and braided my hair into a long plait, the cabin was completely empty.

Or at least, it appeared to be empty. After being caught by Declan, I had no more intentions of snooping around again to make sure that I was, indeed, alone. I tried not to be too discouraged that they'd all left me to deal with figuring things out in the house by myself. No introduction to the kitchen, no 'you can touch this, but not that' with respect to items in the fridge. Nothing.

They were just—gone.

Rather than try and make it to the cafeteria and back to the gym before the hour was up, I found some bread and peanut butter in the pantry that I helped myself to, along with some leftover coffee in a large, steaming black pot on the counter. The second I took a sip, I let out an embarrassingly loud groan. This was, without a doubt, the best coffee I'd ever tasted.

Granted, my typical experience with coffee extended from Cyrus's burnt attempts, the Quickie Mart back home, and the espresso machine in the cafeteria. But still, even in comparison to some artisan shops, I had a feeling this pot held its own.

I could deal with the cold shoulder from Atlas if it meant this level of superb caffeination all the time. Quickly, I filled a spare thermos with some more, prepared to share with Ro once we were at the gym. Looking around the pristine counters, I tried desperately to search for a set of keys.

With a shrug, I locked the door from the inside before leaving, hoping that one of them would be home later to let me in. As I carved my way through the woods, trying to gauge where the Six cabin was in relation to what I understood of Guild grounds so far, nerves crawled along my skin. Alleva was an intimidating woman. It was alarmingly clear where Reza's no-nonsense attitude came from.

Hopefully Alleva would give me a chance, where her daughter did not. I knew that she was generally in charge of training the academy recruits, and I wondered if that meant that Atlas, Dec, and Eli would no longer be training us. And what would that mean for me? I was technically their apprentice now, so would I be expected to continue my class schedule as normal or would I be going on missions as they were assigned them?

A rush of adrenaline flew through my veins at the thought of fighting vampires and werewolves alongside the team. A deep, desperate need to prove myself to them outweighed my general discomfort with their moodiness. Declan was, by far, the most badass girl I had ever encountered, and the thought of getting to shadow her on missions made me downright giddy.

My winding path ended up being severely inaccurate, so by the time I located the gym, I was a few minutes late.

Alleva's attention snapped in my direction as the door

slammed behind me. Her shrewd eyes took in my appearance, lingering here and there as she scanned me.

"Miss Bentley," she bit out, for once making me hate the sound of Cy's last name. "So good of you to join us." Her eyes narrowed, the blue visible through thick, lined lashes. "And so happy that you found time to style your hair and make coffee, rather than show up on time."

My cheeks burned with fire as my eyes fell to Ro and Izzy, grateful for the familiar and warm presence. They both winced slightly, behind small grins, as if my embarrassment had infected them as well.

"I understand that our world is new to you, but your brother," she paused, looking down at her clipboard, too quickly to actually have read anything, "Rowan, made it here on time. Perhaps his manners can be attributed to the fact that he spent half his life living in another household." She cleared her throat, "time will tell."

And then, as if I was nothing more than an annoying gnat, she dismissed me and turned back to the other students.

As silently as possible, I made my way towards the group, wishing desperately that Declan or someone had been around when I left, if only to point me in the right direction or give me some advice on buttering Alleva up.

"As I was saying," she said, her voice crisp and echoing across the room, though the volume wasn't particularly strained. "You will continue your training during typical hours throughout the week, unless your team is scheduled for a mission or specific meeting. On days where that is the case, you will be dismissed from your usual lessons. Make no mistake, however, this will not be an excuse to fall behind on your school work. You will still be held to the same high standards as usual. On evenings where your team doesn't have a specific field assignment, you will spend time bonding with them and getting a feel for what it means to work in a tight-knit group. You will research when they research, train when they train, and learn how to conduct yourselves around Headquarters as a bonafide member of this community."

"What if our teams don't want to bring us along?" Theo, Izzy's older and slightly awful brother asked from the back of the room.

Alleva's mouth straightened into a line, her eyes pinched slightly as she looked down at him with absolute contempt rolling from her in waves. I knew that Theo had a crush on Reza, and I was starting to suspect that her mother wasn't too keen on the idea. Then again, from what I'd seen of Reza and her interactions with Theo, she wasn't too keen on it either.

"I've spoken to the heads of your teams this morning, they all understand that there isn't a choice where this is concerned. Whenever possible, they are to include you, whether they are particularly enthusiastic about it or not." She folded her hands in front of her stomach, straightening up slightly. "Unfortunately, the stakes are too high right now for any of us to consider preference when it comes to decisions about how apprentices should be spending their time." She swept her blue eyes over us, like a queen surveying her loyal subjects. "Now, enough chat. Since you will be losing some valuable training time and since I have missed out on several weeks of observations, you will spend some time today sparring as I walk through and take notes on your progress."

She clapped her hands once and then, as if programmed, the room burst into chaotic energy as students shuffled to available mats, pairing up into their usual groups as quickly as possible.

"Alleva can be a bit of a hardass," Izzy muttered under her breath as she ushered us towards a mat in the center. "She's ruthless, but fair. Just don't get on her bad side," Izzy glanced at me again and I could see my late arrival flashing through her thoughts, "again."

"Ms. Bentley, a word please," Alleva's crisp, clear voice echoed behind me and I spun around so quickly that I sloshed some coffee on the floor.

"Headmistress, I'm really sorry for being late. I got lost between Team Six's cabin and the gym. You have my word it won't happen again."

She nodded once, her stare traveling to the few drops of coffee now coloring my sneakers. "See that it doesn't. I stopped you not to drag that out again but to suggest that you pair up with Reza for this exercise. I've heard great things about your skills during these sessions and I welcome the opportunity to see you execute them against the strongest female in the academy."

Izzy gripped my shoulder in solidarity before grabbing the coffee from my tight fingers and leading Ro towards the mat so that they could get started.

Great.

In my brief time at The Guild, I had sparred with Reza exactly once. And there was nothing about the experience I wanted to experience again. She was a solid fighter, that much was obvious. And I generally respected solid fighters, especially when they were women. Girls had to stick together and all. But when Reza sparred with me, there was an angry intensity in every twitch of her muscle, like it wasn't just an exercise to make us stronger. Like she wanted to leave me weakened, injured, as if to erase me from this place before I could truly leave my imprint on it. And now that I'd taken the spot she wanted with Six, I had a feeling I was in for a whole new level of Reza hate mail.

That kind of negativity was something I didn't have room for.

"Reza," Alleva said, her voice just above a whisper but I had no doubt that every ear in the room was lingering on everything she said. "Come over here and spar with Maxine please. I'd like to see how you've made progress while I've been away."

There was no warmth in her address to her daughter, and as Reza made her way over to us, her long blond hair swaying with each step, I saw a different girl than the one I'd encountered every day since my arrival.

Gone was the confident bully. In her place was a girl shaded red with emotion, shoulders hunched slightly as if to make herself smaller.

"Yes mother," she said, sparing me one quick glance, absent of its usual heat.

Maybe this wouldn't be like our first experience facing off, maybe she'd approach me with the level of detachment most people did in this room—void of personal vendetta.

I followed Reza to the available mat, setting my water bottle and bag down on the ground. We met in the middle with a nod before moving to our separate sides. Reza bounced from heel to heel in her bright pink sneakers, her hands raised and ready to strike.

As soon as Alleva said "go," Reza was rushing towards me, with none of the usual lithe movement I was used to from her. Her steps were clumsy, unsure, and I watched as she glanced out the side of her eyes, like she was trying to observe her mother's reactions in real time. Her fist came flying towards my cheek, broadcasted loudly enough that evading it was easy and effortless.

I spun around, the plush blue mat squeaking against my shoes. I moved towards Reza, feigning left but striking with my fist, twice in the side before pulling back. This time, the familiar heat was reignited across Reza's features, animosity directed towards me like never before. She straightened up, circling around me like we were playing cat and mouse.

This was more like the Reza I was used to seeing on the sparring floor and I glanced briefly at Alleva to see a mildly intrigued, but otherwise unaffected expression on her face.

While Reza's second approach was much more silent than the first, I struck out quickly, swiping her legs out from under her while her focus was on my fists and landing her next hit. She swore softly as the soft thud echoed around us. Kicking her legs up, she jumped back up, ready to go again, but I didn't give her the chance.

In a flash, I had her pinned to the ground again.

And again. And again.

After a particularly gnarly kick to the thigh, I reached a hand out to pull Reza up. With a rough swat, she shoved me away before standing on her own, favoring her left leg just slightly. A renewed rage sparkled in her eyes, like she was visualizing all the ways she wanted to torture me. I had no doubt that each one was more gruesome than the last.

But then she dropped the cold glare and glanced at her mother again, her brows pinching slightly as she rubbed her left wrist against the hem of her pants.

Guilt sunk low in my belly, tightening its hold around my chest like an iron chain.

I wasn't the one Reza was truly upset with. She hated me, sure. But it was a superficial sort of hate. This was something else entirely, something that had almost nothing to do with me.

Alleva walked up to me, sparing her daughter the briefest of glances. "That was well done, Maxine. I'm impressed."

I cringed at the way she said my name, and her tone made it clear that while she might be impressed, she was most definitely not pleased with my arrival here. There was a venom in her expression that chilled me to the bone.

And then, just like that, I was dismissed as she turned on her daughter. "It is enormously clear that in my relatively brief absence, you've let your studies slide. That was one of the worst showings I've seen from you in months. You're being ruled by your emotions, by anger and jealousy. I expect more from my blood and my legacy." Her lip curled in barely-disguised disgust. "What I do not expect is for you to get obliterated by our newest recruit. You should be embarrassed for that showing."

Reza paled significantly, and a rush of empathy coursed through my veins. No wonder Reza was so tightly wound and competitive. Her mother was next-fucking-level intense.

Uncomfortable with encroaching on this moment between mother and daughter, I inched back a few steps at a time until my feet were almost at the edge of the mat. Straightening, I stopped and leveled a stony look at Alleva.

"Reza is actually one of the strongest fighters The Guild has to offer, in my experience, mam. She's the best I've fought at our age group, of that much I'm certain."

As soon as the words left my mouth, I knew that I meant them, surprising even myself. Reza would make one hell of a team member one day, if she could learn to speak to other people without poison eating through her words.

But I'd been training with Cyrus my whole life and with Atlas and his team since my arrival. What's more, my attack outside the bar had renewed my passion for training, my desire to get stronger and move faster. Beating Reza was good, but my ability to best another protector was the least of my concerns. I'd been training to make sure that the next time I came across a hellbeast, I wouldn't need to rely on Ralph or anyone else to come rescue me. Alleva was right, the stakes were too damn high.

My experiences and strengths weren't Reza's fault though and they didn't diminish her own value.

When both women turned in a slow, exaggerated pivot, twin sets of blue piercing into my flesh, I knew that I'd made a mistake. My initial instinct had been right—I should have left them to their own business. Now, Alleva studied me, her temple pulsing slightly as her lip curled in disgust. And then there was Reza.

Steam was practically coming out of her ears and I was half convinced she'd suddenly developed the power to eviscerate me where I stood.

If she hated me before, then I didn't even have a word for the emotion lapping at my skin like sandpaper now.

"Thank you for your astute observation," Alleva bit out, each word punctuated with a full stop. "I am aware of my daughter's strengths, seeing as I have raised her and been in charge of her training throughout her entire life. That is not my issue. My issue is that she's plateaued in her studies." Her long fingers swept an invisible hair back from her face as she smoothed her platinum bob. "More importantly, Ms. Bentley, matters between me and my daughter have absolutely nothing to do with you."

"Yes mam, you're right," I stammered, my heart beating rapidly against my chest. From the corner of my eye, I could see that we were attracting the attention of most of the groups sparring around us. I caught a glimpse of Izzy, her grey eyes rounded with concern. I could tell from her posture that she was warring with herself about whether or not to intervene on my behalf—a realization that thawed some of the ice leveled at me. "I'll leave you both to your conversation."

"Stop," Reza said, halting my retreat as soon as my foot left the mat. "You don't get to infiltrate this place, eavesdrop on private conversations, and ruin my life without answering for it. We go again."

Reza's posture was stiff, her eyes narrowed with the promise of pain. This wasn't about sparring anymore, this was something else. If Alleva came to the same realization, she didn't seem to care. Instead, she nodded to her daughter, as if in approval, before stepping back off the mat. She turned away from us, walking between the other matches, a single look from her enough to get everyone back to sparring with haste.

"Are you sure?" I asked Reza, the words lingering slow and quiet on my tongue.

As an answer, Reza's fist crashed into my nose, a resounding crack ringing through my ears as the taste of copper filled my mouth. For a moment, I was absolutely stunned—this was against everything that Cyrus taught us—there was no waiting for the start, no acknowledged agreement.

Before I could shake myself out of it, Reza punched me in the gut, doubling me over.

"Now, now, Reza, let's fight fair, no face hits," Alleva called across from the gym, her words cold and disapproving, but there was also an odd pride to her tone. Clearly she hadn't seen her daughter throw the punch before the match even started.

I could feel my face caked with blood as I pushed against the mat, trying to catch my grounding through my dry heaves. Reza's foot slammed into my arm, most of her weight being used to keep me down.

"Whoops, that was an accident," she said, as her other foot crashed into my head.

"Reza, enough!" This time Alleva's voice held withering finality, and I saw her jump on the mat to pull her daughter off of me herself. "I'll see you in my office, go there now. We clearly have a lot to discuss."

I felt strong arms pick me up, and the warm, familiar face of Ro appeared above me. Concern shadowed his eyes, my own blood soaking a patch through his shirt. Nosebleeds were a bitch.

"Accidents happen," Alleva said, clearly already bored with the situation. "Tonight, my daughter and I will have a long conversation about cordial sparring. Of that, I can assure you."

I didn't doubt it. We both knew what this was, a momentary reprieve for Reza to defend her honor and seek vengeance for my interference in her life. For beating her in front of her mother, for taking her spot in Six. Not something she'd get away with ever again, but this one time was enough. She'd won this battle.

And I, very clearly, was officially on Alleva's bad side.

"Rowan, take her to the infirmary so that they can set the bones before her nose heals in an unfortunate position. It'd be a shame to permanently mar that pretty face."

10

MAX

Getting bones reset was always worse than breaking them in the first place. Maybe because the offending spot was already screaming something awful at you in terms of pain receptors. Maybe because you knew it was coming in a way that you probably didn't know with the initial break. Probably both.

All I knew was that my brief excitement about seeing my favorite nurse—Greta—almost instantly deflated as soon as she looked at me with those wise, wrinkly eyes, laced with pity and empathy.

After fixing my nose and assessing my arm and the rest of my face, she gripped my shoulder in her warm hand, pushing me back against the pillow.

"Seems we are destined to keep meeting like this, Ms. Bentley. Damn shame." Her wild gray hair flapped slightly as she shook her head. "We medical workers go into the business of helping people, but that tends to mean we only interact with them when they need help."

"Thanks for fixing me up, Greta," I grumbled, feeling guilty for the barrage of elaborate cursing she had to suffer through a few moments ago. "I appreciate it."

A large smile carved across her face as she turned to Ro. "You go on and get back to your classes, Mr. Bentley. This isn't like last time. Just a quick break. She'll be up and out of here in a couple hours or so. She just needs some rest."

Ro grumbled a bit, but even he was incapable of arguing with the headstrong nurse. After making me promise I'd text him when I left the infirmary, he reluctantly left.

"Thanks for that too," I grunted, pushing myself up into more of a seated position. "Ever since the attack at Vanish, he gets that worried mother hen look on his face whenever I'm hurt now. It's like he's terrified any little thing will result in my permanent demise." I winked at her playfully. "But if I can take on a vamp and live to tell the tale, then Reza's fist doesn't stand a chance."

"Ah well, go easy on the boy. You scared him last time you were brought in here. You missed it, being unconscious and all, but he was in a frenzied state, let me tell you. Bringing you back down to visit me probably just dredged all that up a bit, is all. Give him time."

She brought a wet rag over to help me wipe up some of the blood that had dried and crusted on my arm. Unfortunately, my sports bra would be soaked until I could get it home and in the wash. All of a sudden, I remembered that when I'd be leaving here, I'd be going back to the cabin with Six. Did they have a laundry room? I hadn't exactly gotten a tour. Hell, I still didn't even have a damn key.

Greta wiggled her nose a bit as she moved some things over on my tray. Mischief played out across her eyes as she studied me. "I had to get a new key card you know. Seems I lost mine around the last time you visited me. Damn shame. Hopefully it didn't end up in the wrong hands."

I started to grin, but reined it in at the last minute. My face felt like it had been bulldozed by a truck, so it was in my best interest to limit my expressiveness until the bones healed up a bit. "Damn shame," I echoed.

She let out a harsh, raspy chuckle before moving towards the door. "It's not your first broken bone, I'm sure, so you know the deal. Try and rest a bit for a couple hours until the bulk of the pain is gone, then you're free to go and return to your Saturday plans. If I remember correctly, you have quite the way with healing, so I'm sure you'll be right as rain in record time."

I never understood that phrase, right as rain. But it echoed through my thoughts as I dozed in and out for a couple hours. Better that and Greta's oddly musical laugh than all the ways I was going to make Reza pay.

When I came to, I felt almost completely healed. While Greta had been talking about my almost miraculous healing from a vampire bite, I had never been a particularly fast healer—not nearly as fast as Ro anyway. Hell, even after that attack, while my vamp wounds vanished quickly, my other injuries from that night took a hell of a lot longer.

Not this time, though. Carefully, I pressed my fingers into the skin on my face, walking my hands across the bridge of my nose, my forehead, and orbital bones.

No pain.

My nose was still crusted with dried blood, and I probably still had some bruising coloring my skin, but otherwise I felt completely normal. Maybe it was because I was getting so close to my nineteenth birthday—the year when I would 'officially' come into my protector power and be an adult in this community.

If it meant I wouldn't have to live with injuries for as long as I'd had to in the past, then I was all about getting older.

I jumped out of bed, sliding my shirt over my sports bra and stretching my arms from side to side, getting rid of any leftover stiffness from the fight. My bag was settled on a chair near my bed and I let out a sigh of gratitude for Ro. He'd managed to collect it, along with me, on his way to depositing me at Greta's door.

Generally, I wouldn't care much about having my stuff with

me, but these days I never left my room without making sure that Greta's keycard was somewhere close by—either tucked into my leggings or else stashed in my gym bag.

The room was cast in shadow, the hallway much quieter than it had been when I'd arrived. If I had to guess, I'd say we were getting close to dinner time, so most people were probably camped back at their rooms or else in the cafeteria filling up on some food.

A flickering light danced in the hallway, casting the floor in a cadence of shadows. I made my way a few doors down, before making sure I was truly alone. I wasn't exactly clear on what the visiting hours were in the infirmary, and I didn't want to get on Greta's bad side. She'd proven herself to be more than formidable. Hell, the first time I'd encountered her, she'd had even Atlas listening and catering to every demand.

Satisfied that I was indeed alone, I pushed my way into the room. A gentle whir of machine buzzing filled my ears as I crept closer to the bed. He was still, like he was trapped in nothing more than a pleasant dream, his chest moving up and down to the rhythm of my own.

There was a chair on the left side of his bed, one that I'm sure Atlas had spent countless nights dozing in as he stood guard over his brother, desperate for him to snap out of whatever sort of hold had his mind trapped.

I sat down, carefully reaching for Wade's hand, the skin smooth against my own, save for a few calluses he'd earned from weapons work.

"I miss you," I muttered, feeling slightly ridiculous for talking to a man in a coma—and one I only barely knew, really. Except for some reason, even though his presence in my life had been brief, I felt like he was a part of me—destined to be a big part of my life. Other than Izzy, he was probably my first friend here, the first one to really make me feel comfortable. Safe.

I reached up to his face, taking advantage of the fact that I was alone, sweeping his cheek gently with my thumb. Smooth, brown skin, deceptively soft.

The machine nearest me jumped slightly, the beeping speeding up. I sat up, looking around the room before turning back to Wade. Was that normal?

After a moment, the machine settled back down to the familiar *bu-bump* it'd been singing since the second I opened the door.

A long yawn pulled from my mouth, a sudden wave of exhaustion creeping over me. Greta told me to stay down here for as long I needed rest, but she didn't necessarily say that the rest had to occur in my room.

Butt in the chair, I scooched closer to Wade's bed until I could comfortably lean down and rest my head on the firm block that passed as a mattress down here. Slowly at first, and then all at once, sleep pulled me under.

When my eyes opened, I was standing inside a large entryway, the walls decorated in lavish webs of gold and silver. A soft glow washed over the room, the gradual flickering reminiscent of a symphony of candles, though I couldn't see any from where I stood.

I took a step forward as a tendril of silk brushed against my calf. Looking down, I saw that I was dressed in a deep red gown, the color warming the tan shade of my skin. With a steady hand, I touched my hair, noticing the heavy locks were brandished up in a complex series of knots and braids.

Soft, instrumental music echoed down the hall, and I followed the sound at a leisurely pace. I wasn't entirely sure where I was, but something about this place felt familiar, right, somehow. Wherever I was going, I didn't feel rushed or hurried.

Turning down the long hall, I walked up to a large double set of doors, the wood thick and heavy enough that I had to exert force to open them. Before me, more gold and silver decorated the ballroom, with complex paintings winding around the walls and ceiling.

It was odd, but the place was both empty and full of people. Each time I tried to look at a face, the individual vanished, replaced by another faceless shadow, and then another.

"You're here," a soft, deep voice said from behind me. There was familiarity in the tone, and even a hesitant fear. "You shouldn't be here."

I turned around and was met with a pair of cool, blue eyes.

Wade.

The soft glow of the room brought a renewed warmth to his skin, though his eyes were heavy, like he hadn't slept in days. Like me, he was dressed for some peculiarly lavish affair, head-to-toe in rich black with accents of textured gold.

"Where is here, exactly?" I asked, closing the distance between us until we were barely a foot apart. The rush of phantoms around us all but sunk back into the background, as if they'd done their part in uniting us and could now rest.

Wade's eyes narrowed slightly in frustration, a wrinkle forming between his brows. Without hesitation, I reached my thumb up to smooth it away.

"I don't really know, I've been trying to figure it out. I've seen pictures of this place before. I think—I think this is where my parents met."

My eyes bent in curiosity as I took in the odd, almost Victorian setting around us. "Really? What makes you say that?" The details of the room were simultaneously vibrant and unclear, like I could only focus on isolated parts. "Something feels off, here."

"I don't really know, I just have a feeling." His hand dropped to mine, our skin touching in a wave of heat so strong that I only then realized I must have been freezing. A rush of chill swept down my spine and I clung to his hand like I needed his touch in order to breathe.

"This place is odd," I said. "Something doesn't feel right."

We stood in silence for a long second, the whirlwind of the room, filled with strange visions and shadows, moving around us like we were in an odd snow globe.

"I think you're right. I hadn't noticed that before. Somehow it seemed...normal or familiar."

I closed my eyes, trying to ground myself. Where had I been before I was here? What was I doing?

"Reza," I mumbled. I had been fighting with Reza.

"Reza? Do you see her somewhere?" Wade's eyes studied me with a ferocious intensity, like his gaze was magnetized to mine.

I shook my head, frowning. "No, I was just sparring with her in the gym." I paused, thinking harder now, trying to trace my time. "And then I was with Greta and Ro in the infirmary." My fingers gripped Wade's with a sudden desperation. "Oh."

"Oh?" he echoed, worry lacing his tone like he was mirroring mine.

"I'm dreaming." It came back in a rush, all at once: that Wade was injured, still in a coma. He wasn't here with me, not really. "After I healed, I walked to your room. You've been asleep since your team's last mission. You were attacked. I must have drifted off to sleep, you the last thing on my mind."

The warmth of his fingers was vibrant now, filled with the grounding reality of my body on the other side of this dream—where our hands really touched.

"Attacked? That makes sense, I suppose," though he said it like he didn't really believe it. "If this is your dream, does that mean I'm not real? That this is all just in your head?"

Something about the way he said it created a small fissure in my chest, and I wished for a long moment that it wasn't true. That I would wake up and Wade's smiling face would greet me. That his attack hadn't happened.

My silence was answer enough, so he just nodded, strong determination squaring his jaw. "I see. Well, all the same, real me will be happy to know I've made a feature in your dreams at least."

Several, if I was being honest with myself.

He looked down at me, his eyes teasing. "And since this isn't real, I think that means it's okay if I do this."

"Do wh—"

His lips crashed against mine, warm and soft and firm. We held onto each other like a knot, desperately trying not to come undone.

My breath pulsed heavily, and Wade pulled back, his eyes studying me with renewed curiosity.

"Bentley."

The voice wasn't Wade's, but it wasn't unfamiliar either.

"Bentley, wake up."

Wade pressed a kiss to my forehead. "You should go. Thank you, Max. Even if I'm just in your head, I'm grateful that I was able to do that just this once."

"Bentley!"

My breath pulled out of me in a rush and I went crashing to the floor, my fingers letting go of Wade's on the way down.

"You have a habit of having intense dreams in this wing," Atlas said, his tall figure towering over me, shielding me slightly from the fluorescent lighting of the ceiling.

The dream came back to me in a rush and when I looked up at Wade, my heart fell to my stomach. Just as he was before, he was completely still, eyes shut and still in a coma.

"He's still not up?" I asked.

Atlas cocked a brow, like that was the most obtuse question he'd heard, but then his expression softened. "No. Still not up."

A long, awkward pause fell between us, both of us likely lost in our own anxieties about Wade.

"And they still don't know when he'll wake up?"

Atlas shook his head, his throat bobbing slightly like he was trying to find words or the courage to say them, but couldn't.

He pulled up another chair, the blue cushion cracked and worn with use, before sitting on the other side of Wade.

I wasn't sure how long we sat like that, it could have been seconds or hours, but eventually, I found myself studying Atlas with just as much focus as I studied Wade's peaceful face. The similarities were subtle, but in this moment, they were there. In the strong edges of Atlas's jaw, the shape of his eyes. When Atlas was like this—vulnerable and concerned, rather than apathetic or angry—it was easier to imagine them as brothers. I hadn't seen it before, but I saw it now.

His dark eyes met mine, and I could see the shadings of gold that were sometimes visible in certain lighting. As if the observation of his vulnerability was enough to shatter it, he stood straighter, his face freezing back into that impenetrable shield of his.

"You shouldn't be down here." There was a rawness to his voice, almost an anger. It felt for a moment, like he was mad at me for witnessing him unraveled, however briefly.

"I was already down here," I said, not sure if he'd heard about the fight earlier. "Your girlfriend broke my nose. I thought I might as well stop by and visit Wade before going back to the cabin." I cleared my throat and stared back, unwilling to break our eye contact first.

His nostrils flared and I watched as his jaw muscles tensed while he worked out whatever it was he was going to respond with. Instead, he fished around in his pocket before tossing a key at me. "That's mine. I'll want it back. Go back to the cabin now."

The key was on a single circular ring, but there were no keychains or personal trinkets. For a moment, I wondered if everything in Atlas's life was like this—cold, impersonal, transient.

I opened my mouth to argue, but when I met his eyes again, there was a fire there, like one more moment stuck in here with me would make him explode with anger.

Rather than wait to find out, I nodded once before pocketing the key and standing. I leaned down, pressing a soft kiss on Wade's cheek and giving his hand one gentle squeeze.

"Until I dream again," I muttered, ignoring Atlas's scowl, before turning back to the door and leaving the room.

I would go back to the cabin—I couldn't quite bring myself to call it home—eventually. First, I wanted to stop by and check on Ralph, since I was already down here.

The halls were quieter than usual as I made my way through the small maze. I took a wrong turn at some point though, and found myself at a dead-end. I blamed it on a combination of my recent injury and exhaustion. The dream with Wade had felt anything but restful.

FORGING THE GUILD

When I reached a key entry, I waved Greta's card, though I was fairly certain this wasn't the way I usually came when visiting Ralph.

With a satisfying click, the door opened, a bright light revealing an impeccably clean room filled with white walls and various metal instruments. A quick glance told me that I was alone, so I stepped inside, suddenly desperate to understand what went on down here. Was this one of the rooms that Ralph had to undergo his tests in?

A long counter ran the length of the room, filled with all sorts of jars of liquid and unfriendly instruments. My fingers swept along the edge of one particularly angry-looking metal knife. I picked it up until a loud *clank* startled me enough that I dropped it to the ground—a soft, tinny reverberation echoed through the room.

When I spun around, I exhaled sharply. I wasn't as alone as I'd thought.

Lying on the other end of the room was a woman strapped to a long metal bed. She was strapped at the wrists and ankles, with a particularly thick metal band wrapping around her forehead and waist to keep her in place.

She looked so small, and young. She couldn't be older than eleven if I had to guess, judging by her height and her soft plump skin. Long blond hair was drooping across the side of the bed, the strands stringy like they hadn't been brushed or cleaned in months.

"Help," she said, her voice quiet and doll-like, as she tried desperately to get a better look at me with her head restrained. She had eyes to match the voice: large and round, like a scared doe.

"Who are you?" I asked, my voice coming out in a croak. I needed to leave, I knew that I needed to leave. But for some reason, against my better judgment, I took a step closer to her and then another.

"Please, you have to help me." A single tear slid from her eye, carving a curved line down her face and disappearing into her hair. "They're going to kill me."

"What are you?" I asked, changing my question just slightly.

Now that I was closer, she looked less like a child and more like a regular girl—nothing about her seemed terrifying or strong. Instead, she was broken and thin and trembling with fear. Whatever she was, she desperately believed that she was going to die. When I reached no more than a foot away, she visibly flinched away from me, closing her eyes like I might strike.

Her nostrils flared until her doll-eyes sprang back open, wider even than they were before.

"Blood."

She pulled against her restraints, trying to reach me, to get me into her sights.

"Blood. It's so strong."

She bared her teeth, showing two long fangs and I jumped back, knocking into another table and sending various instruments clattering to the ground.

"Get the fuck out of here." Atlas was framed in the doorway I'd just been standing in. "Now."

Shit.

11
MAX

I realized instantly that whatever was going through Atlas's thoughts when I was in Wade's room was not anger. This. Right now. This was anger. In fact, I'd never seen him angry until now.

His sharp, dark eyes radiated heat as he strode into the room, gripping my arm with a strength that would surely bruise me. Without another word of protest, we left the crying girl alone in the room and made our way out of the lab wing.

As we wove through the halls with a crisp precision, Atlas stayed silent. He pulled me along behind him, walking so quickly that between his speed and my height, my feet were practically gliding above the floors.

"I'm sorry," I mumbled, for the first time legitimately afraid of Atlas. "I was trying to see Ralph, and I lost my focus and made a bad turn."

Nothing.

"That girl. She was a vampire. And so young," I tried again.

Nothing. Though I hadn't asked a question, I doubt he would've acknowledged me if I had.

I knew that vampires were born, not made. But still, it had never dawned on me that there were children. What's more, it had never dawned on me that The Guild would be experimenting on children. I'd never seen anything like it, such a perfect mixture of deadly power and innocence. Part of me had been so moved to help her, just a breath away from loosening her restraints. But then, the way that she looked at me, studying my neck with a ferocious, dangerous hunger—I had no doubt that if she was free, she would have tried to kill me.

With my free hand I gripped at my shirt, remembering belatedly that my clothes were still soaked in my blood. Had she been starved? Was that why she was so focused on me once she caught my scent?

I thought back to my discussion with Declan, when she'd come to my suite to watch films with me, Ro, and Izzy. She'd mentioned that the vampires in the labs were some of the most dangerous creatures housed in The Guild. That they only kept the most powerful, the most important to study and learn from.

But a child. Was she really as dangerous as most vampires? Could she have out-fought me the way the vampire at the club had?

Yes. Remembering the determination, the combination of fear and hunger and desperation in her eyes. There was a rabid determination in her, so different from the equally terrifying vampire across from Ralph's prison. Where he seemed all cold edges and feral power, even with his teasing, sing-song challenges, she was unrestrained energy, waiting to combust.

"Hello Atlas," a girl with wild red hair greeted as we made our way through the ground level of the mansion. She was beautiful, and closer to his age than to mine, so I assumed she must either belong to a team or else work on campus somewhere. Her sharply carved brows bent in the middle as we moved closer towards her. "You okay? Something wrong? Has Wade—"

Atlas passed her without so much as breaking his stride, pulling me towards another endless hallway. I looked back, frowning slightly in apology at the girl as she stood in stupefied curiosity behind us.

I was all but running now, trying to keep up with him as he pulled me along towards whichever destination he was aiming for. My arm was almost numb from his grip.

"Will they kill her?" I asked, and I wasn't sure which answer I wanted to hear. Frustrated now that he was still carting me along like a heavy purse, I shoved the heel of my palm into his back, trying to break him out of whatever obnoxious alpha anger thing he had going on. "Hey. I'm not a fucking doll. If you want to yell at me for being down there or whatever, then yell at me. But don't manhandle me through the entire Guild Headquarters while ignoring me and every single person we pass."

He stilled, turning into a statue so quickly that I didn't have time to adjust my speed without crashing into him. He didn't so much as budge while I flopped awkwardly against him, my cheek ramming into his granite back.

I stood there for a moment, waiting for him to say something or let go of me or look at me. Just...something.

And then when he did react, I almost wished he hadn't. That I had just let him storm off, swinging me around helplessly after him until we were in the cabin and I could hide, properly-chastised, behind my door.

Instead, with cool, calm precision, he turned his neck to the right until his face leveled with a dark door. He shoved his way through and I spilled into an empty classroom filled with abandoned desks and old papers.

He shut the door behind us, not a moment after my foot crossed the threshold, and spun me so that my back pressed against the glossed wood. Long, lean muscles caged me in, his hands gripping on each of my shoulders now. He didn't need to use any pressure, I wouldn't have budged from this spot of my own volition. Blood was swirling through my veins so fast that my ears were filled with the sound.

With a steady breath, I tried to compose my racing heart and looked up at him, meeting his fiery gaze. His brown eyes looked almost yellow when I was up this close. Less than a few inches separated my face from his. And I stared at the way his nostrils flared softly every time air passed through his lungs, like he had to remind himself to breathe.

"Atlas? Are you—"

"You don't listen do you?"

"I—"

"Like, ever. You never listen. You do what you want, when you want, and you don't give a fuck who it screws over in the mean time, even if the person getting screwed over is you."

"I—"

"I mean, you've been in our world for what? A couple of weeks? And how many times have you almost gotten yourself killed? You do understand that you were in a room with a vampire? By yourself. And instead of leaving as soon as you realized where you were and what kind of situation you were in, you walked *towards* the vampire like you had a fucking deathwish. Who walks towards a vampire without a team of protection at their back? All of this, minutes after you had promised me you'd go home?"

In all of my time training with him, I think this was the most I had ever heard him speak. And for once, I was hoping he shared his thoughts and feelings less.

"Technically, I didn't promise I was going back to the cabin, you just asked me...to," I said, almost instantly regretting that of all the sentences he'd allowed me to finish, that was the one we were stuck with.

A long, intense silence drew out between us and all I could think about was the fact that we were standing so close together that we were both probably inhaling each other's exhales in an oddly intimate sort of suffocation.

His eyes narrowed, the edges of his glare sharp enough to skin me alive. A low, deep rumbling sound reverberated in his chest and I briefly wondered if he was in fact a vampire with the way he was suddenly looking at me like he wanted to bite off my head.

"I'm sorry, okay. I should have left the room as soon as I realized what she was," I said, no longer able to stand the silent standoff. "But I'm not sorry for trying to check on Ralph. Because whether anyone cares or not, when I was last up against a vampire, he was the one who had my back. He's my team."

I paused, suddenly filled with the rightness of that sentiment. I trusted Ralph completely. And if it weren't for him—twice now—I would be dead.

"And," I continued, my spine straightening with growing confidence, "while it would have been my fault if I were attacked just now, the same isn't true for the vamp attack outside of Vanish or the wolf attack back in my hometown. Neither of those situations were my fault. It's the fucking twenty-first century. Don't blame the victim. And furthermore, while I appreciate the fact that you thought I was in some sort of real danger against an immobilized baby vamp, I would appreciate it more if your way of handling it didn't consist of dragging me about like a damn suitcase, bruising my arm, or jumping down my throat. Sort of ruins the archaic heroism trope you were probably trying to go for."

As if he was stunned, and only just now coming to, his eyes widened until they almost resembled the little girl's. He glanced down at his hands, at the way they pressed me into the door, and dropped them like I'd burned him. In a flash, he was halfway across the room like he was trying to put as much distance between us as possible.

He opened his mouth to speak, but we were interrupted by a loud knocking on the other side of my skull.

"Atlas, Max, that you? What's all the yelling about?" Eli's deep voice crept through the wood and I stepped away from the door so that I could let him inside. "Jesus, you alright, Max? Look a little worse for wear. I heard about the whole situation with Reza this morning."

This morning? Had it really been such a short while ago? It

felt like it had been days since I was lying back on a gurney while Greta reset my nose in a symphony of painful movements.

"I'm fine," I said, the bravado drained from my voice now. "How did you know we were in here?"

Eli's dark brow arched into a crisp peak, his eyes traveling between me and Atlas with a teasing curiosity. "Am I interrupting something?"

"I got your text about boundary patrol and went to find her so that she could join us," Atlas said, his voice gruff and laced with just a hint of the anger he'd unloaded on me moments before.

So that's why he'd left his brother so quickly. He must've followed me.

"Boundary patrol?" I asked, directing my question to Eli and trying desperately to ignore Atlas behind me. I wasn't successful though. I could feel his eyes boring into my back like a pair of sharp daggers.

"Yeah," Eli said, dragging the word out as he met Atlas's glare. "Alleva had a conversation with all of the teams today, wants to make sure the apprentices are properly shadowing whenever possible. And I just got word about half an hour ago that our group is on boundary patrol. A team has been taking patrol once a night since the attack near headquarters. Just to be safe and to monitor for any suspicious activities or signs of other beasts getting too close to where we all eat, shit, and sleep, you know?"

"And I get to come?" I asked, slightly annoyed with myself for how eager I sounded.

"You do, gorgeous. We can split up and you can take my half of campus." He nodded to Atlas who was still stewing silently behind me. "Cool with you if you and Dec team up?"

He grunted a response that I guess could be considered an adjacent yes before leaving the room without so much as glancing back at me once.

"He okay?" Eli pointed his thumb behind him, a shadow of anxiety across his face. "He seems even more surly than usual."

I exhaled, hard enough to send a few stray hairs flying around my face, before walking out the door and following Eli's stride towards wherever it was we were going. "He caught me downstairs trying to see Ralph, but I accidentally wound up in a room with a child vampire, so he dragged me all the way up here like a caveman. And then when he yelled at me, I called his attitude out and—boom—extra surly Atlas."

A low, warm chuckle filled Eli's chest and he swung his arm over my shoulders, the weight heavy in a comforting way, as we marched. "You're a blast to have a round, you know that? I would pay good money to watch somebody tell Atlas off. I don't think it's ever been done before, not really."

While it was a weird thing to be complimented for, I found myself smiling slightly. I hadn't really had to set boundaries before and it felt good to stand up for myself. I shouldn't have been in that part of the research labs, sure. But that didn't give Atlas permission to be an asshole.

"So," I started, shaking off any lingering discomfort about my conversation with the leader of Six, "what exactly does boundary patrol entail?"

"Unfortunately, it's not particularly exciting. We'll walk around and through the grounds to see if anything looks suspicious. We won't find anything, of course, but it's good to be proactive with the increase in attacks. Plus, this time of year it's actually kind of peaceful. The rest of campus is tucked inside, so it's just you and the great outdoors, wandering through the woods and listening to the sounds."

When he put it that way, it didn't sound too bad. "Do we have time to swing by the cabin? I'd like to grab a jacket." It also wasn't lost on me that I was still wearing a sports bra crusted over with blood, but I didn't want to postpone our duties too long—a shower would have to wait unfortunately.

Eli shrugged out of his hunter green zip-up hoodie and

draped it around me. A warm, intoxicating scent filled my nose, and I shivered at the way his body heat still lingered in the fabric.

"Won't you be cold?" I asked, hoping like hell that it was too dark outside for him to see the blush covering my cheeks.

"Nah, I run hot," he said, with an exaggerated wink. "Now that we have a pleasantly long walk ahead of us, you can spill all the details on your fight with Reza and how you kicked Atlas's ass."

"I didn't kick Atlas's ass," I said, rolling my eyes but grinning nonetheless.

"Hey, a guy can dream."

I filled him in on Headmistress Alleva's chilly disposition towards her daughter, catching a thoughtful, almost sad look on Eli's face several times during that part of the story. I wanted to ask what he was thinking about, but Eli seemed quieter than usual, more interested in just listening to me as we carved our chaotic path through the trees.

He was surprisingly easy to talk to, so I mentioned my dream with Wade and happening upon the girl in the lab. He took in every detail with rapt attention, like every syllable I uttered was of utmost importance to him.

Eventually, we made our way to a familiar spot.

"Your lake," I said, my voice low and hushed as I walked up to the large pond and studied the way the moon reflected onto the obsidian glass-like water. It was just as peaceful as I'd remembered—maybe even more so after such a turmoil-filled day. I watched as small fish created tiny ripples of concentric circles, as the gentle breeze blew wind and debris around my feet. "I forgot how beautiful it was."

Warmth spread through my right hand and I looked down to see Eli's fingers laced with mine. He didn't say anything for a long moment, but he pulled me down to the ground so that we were seated together, my side pressed up against his like we were glued.

I contemplated the way that he watched the water. So much focus, so much awe. But underneath it all, there was a layer of something nefarious, something dark, like he was being haunted by something, my hand an anchor keeping him grounded.

"When my mother left us, this is where I would come. Every night, for months, I'd sit out here and try to imagine the places that she was traveling through, the monsters she was fighting. I tried to imagine what kind of life she was living, what kind of life would take her away from us. It had to be great, right?" His voice was so soft, nothing more than a whisper, and I held my breath as he spoke. Tightening my hold on his hand so that he knew that I was here, that I was listening. "I snuck out successfully for weeks, until one night my father stopped by my room but couldn't find me. He went sick with worry, waking up every member of his old team, trying desperately to figure out where I'd gone." He took a heavy breath in, his teeth worrying over his bottom lip. "He told me years ago that he thought I'd left too, that my mother had come back in the dead of night to steal me away, to make his isolation complete. Eventually, of course, he found me here. And for weeks, we'd meet here and sit, until it was so late we couldn't tell if it was night still or if the day had crossed into morning.

"He doesn't come back here often, not for the last couple years anyway. But it's still our spot, still the space where the world goes quiet, just a little, just for a moment."

"I'm sorry," I said, even though I hated when people said that —apologized as if that would bring the person they missed back, provide some balm for an impossible wound. But it was all I could think to say.

At first. Because in some ways, it was a familiar story.

"Sometimes," I started, "when I was growing up, I would imagine that my mother—wherever she was—was living these grand adventures, or that she was kidnapped by rogues, waiting for me to save her. When Ro moved in, he'd build the stories with me, until eventually we had this whole mythology about who she was, and why she'd left me with Cyrus. Never once did he allow me to sink into the despair that she was dead, or that she simply didn't want me. He couldn't stand me feeling that pain, dealing with the heavy agony he went through when his own parents died."

"What was your favorite story you dreamed up about her?" Eli asked, leaning his weight against me like I was his wall, built for no other reason than to keep him steady.

I shrugged, turning to face him once more, focused on the way his eyes transitioned from brown to amber. "I don't remember any of them. Because while those stories were necessary for me at one point, eventually, in building them, Ro became my family. And I didn't need them anymore. Didn't need to know what happened to her or why she left. I just needed him —just Ro and Cyrus. And before I knew it, I was happy. And I felt safe. Loved, even."

It felt strange, to say these things out loud, to whisper them into the dark with a boy I barely knew, with a boy who typically seemed so focused on using his cheekiness to keep people at arm's length. But Eli was different here. He was stripped down somehow. And after his story, after showing me his own wound, it seemed like the thing to do—to offer my own for him to see.

I looked down—for no longer than a moment—to stare at the way our hands knotted together, to soothe the fluttering in my stomach. When I looked back up, Eli's face was several inches closer to mine. He looked into my eyes with a heady focus, a silent question in his eyes.

And when he found the answer he was looking for, he closed the distance between us, until his lips were hugging mine, skin against skin.

His tongue pressed against my bottom lip and I gasped in surprise—an invitation for Eli to deepen the kiss. A heavy weight started to build in my chest, like a grip against my ribs, and I matched every stroke of his tongue with one of my own as we eagerly learned the feel and taste of each other. His left hand moved behind my back, drawing me closer to him, as his right snaked up my arm and tangled itself into my hair. I could feel the light sting of him ripping a strand or two out as he tried to reposition himself, a sensation that strangely sent a tingling feeling through my body. He bit my lip softly between his teeth, creating an intoxicating blend of pleasure and pain. I gasped into his mouth, and he swallowed it eagerly, until a low groan seemed to climb up his chest.

Wanting to reposition myself, I opened my eyes, just a crack, and every muscle in my body froze.

Bright yellow eyes peered out at me from between the trees behind us and I could just make out the large, beastly shape of a wolf.

Noticing my stillness, Eli stopped and pulled away, his lips plump and red, his eyes glazed with lust. "What's wrong? Was that too much?"

"The wolf," I said, pointing behind him. "It's real."

Fast as lightning, Eli spun around and stood, every muscle in his body edged with tension. "Where?"

I looked into the woods, staring at the yellow eyes, and when I opened my mouth again, they were gone. "It was just there. You didn't see it?"

"No, I didn't see it," he echoed, his voice distant, like he was distracted all of a sudden. "Must've been a play of light or maybe you saw just a regular wolf. They're known to go through these parts on occasion."

"No I—" I thought back, to the first werewolf I'd seen. I was sure this one looked like that one. That it was real and not some figment of my imagination.

"No, Max. There's nothing there. I don't hear anything large stirring in the trees. You've had a long day, it's possible your body is just exhausted from healing and then—" He didn't finish the sentence, letting the memory of our kiss linger. His eyes dropped from mine, as he stared at the grass. "I'm sorry, we shouldn't have—I, I shouldn't have done that. Do you forgive me? Can we just forget it happened?"

Stunned, I nodded. Did he not feel that? How good we fit, locked together like that?

A small, sad smile tipped the corner of his lips and something in his eyes flayed me alive.

Regret.

He wished that we didn't kiss. Hell, he probably wished he didn't tell me about his mom either. About this place.

He shoved his hand into his pocket and turned around. "We should go."

A loud rustling filled our quiet scene, as I tried to untangle the past few minutes into something that was familiar, that made sense.

Declan emerged from the trees, her piercing green eyes studying Eli with complete concentration, like the two were locked in a silent conversation or battle.

"It's clear out here," she said, her words crisp and cold, like steel. "Atlas said we can head back home after another round."

Without so much as looking back at me, Eli walked towards her. "Dec, why don't you take Max for the last pass, I have to go take care of something but we'll talk later."

12

MAX

My nightmares were filled with a pair of vibrant, yellow eyes stalking my every move. And when I woke up the next day, the house was filled with a chilling silence. Stretching, I walked to the door to search for everyone, but all that I found was a hasty note taped to my door. No information, other than the fact that they had protector business to handle today and I was to stay out of trouble and be home by nightfall.

Who the hell did they think they were?

Be home by nightfall.

I wasn't a child. And why didn't anyone wake me and ask me to join them? Alleva made it abundantly clear yesterday that we were supposed to accompany our teams on all protector business, whenever possible. That's the only way we were going to learn—by observing and doing. It was Sunday, not like I had anything else to do with my time. And the last thing I needed was another reason to be on Alleva's bad side.

My stomach tightened with the weight of a heavy ball at the thought of last night. Had Eli mentioned the wolf? Did he really think I was seeing things? Were they afraid that I wasn't good enough—capable enough? That I couldn't be taken seriously?

Too many of those possibilities rang with an unsettling truth that made me itch with discomfort.

And I wouldn't let myself so much as think about the kiss, or the way I fell asleep with the soothing tingle of Eli's lips still on my skin. As if things weren't already awkward and tense enough in this house as it was. Boundary crossing created a whole next level of complexity. And between Eli's direct rejection after the kiss and Declan's almost silent patrol following it, I didn't think I could handle much more emotional whiplash where Six was concerned. If the three of them weren't already begging Alleva to kick me out, I had a feeling they would be soon.

I took a deep breath in and out, trying to practice some of the meditation techniques Cy was always rambling about. They never worked on me. My mind was an annoying beast that wouldn't shut the fuck up half the time.

Fuming, I crinkled the paper into a ball and tossed it into the hallway, happy to let them find it. Generally, I wasn't a very passive aggressive person, but in my current mood, I was willing to make an exception.

I left the house, in search of Ro or Izzy. If my team wasn't going to include me in whatever they were doing today, maybe theirs would. I didn't want to sound needy, but wasn't the whole point of this apprenticeship that we were supposed to shadow our teams and learn from them?

I found Izzy, Ro, and the rest of the members of Ten sitting at our usual breakfast table and I clamped down on the jealousy pooling in my belly. My eyes briefly lingered on the table where Atlas and his team usually sat, but they weren't there. After piling my plate high with eggs, bacon, and some pancakes, I sat down with the group, letting myself be enveloped by the positive vibes radiating from Izzy and Sharla.

They were planning a movie night for later this week and invited me along. For a moment, I thought about seeing if Declan was interested in coming by too, before remembering that she didn't seem to want to be around me at all. Which sucked, because she seemed to fit in great when she came to our last one. She got along well with Izzy and was able to dish out witty movie commentary just as quickly as Ro. What had changed since then to suddenly make her so distant?

All of a sudden, as if my body could sense the tension, I turned around and saw Cyrus and Seamus in what looked like a heated argument with a man. He was short and rather stocky for a protector, and his body was draped in what appeared to be a large lab coat. Though it was thinning on top, something about his deep red hair seemed familiar. His posture was stiff and haughty, which surprised me. I'd be buckling under Cyrus's mood if I was him.

Nothing about Cyrus's stance and tense face probably read as unusual to most of the people in the room. He was generally a pretty standoffish guy and I hadn't seen him around too many protectors other than his brother since we arrived. But there was something lethal in his stance now, in the stillness surrounding him. It was like every nerve in his body was on edge, frayed somehow.

I didn't know Seamus very well, but his body language matched his brother's like a mirror, inch for inch.

Something was off. I'd shared a house with the man nearly every day of my entire life and pissed him off more times than I could count—daily. The level of anger radiating around him was like nothing I'd ever been on the receiving end of before.

Who was he talking to?

"Dear old dad," Jer said, as if I'd asked the question out loud. The heat of his breath brushed against the shell of my ear. I pushed back a few inches, not comfortable with the proximity, but he didn't seem to notice. A darkness sank into his normally playful eyes, his posture more rigid than usual. The familiarity of the man's hair made sense now.

In all the hours I'd spent around Jer, which had been considerable over the last few weeks, this was the first time his expression was anything but laid back, flirty, or friendly.

"I take it you don't get along," I said, cocking an eyebrow. I was intrigued to know the details but didn't want to pry. Family stuff could be tricky.

"That's putting it lightly," Sharla said, her curls bouncing as she laughed at something Arnell said to her right. She continued speaking to Jer, but I more or less tuned them out, trying to discreetly study the older protectors without craning my neck too obviously. Stealth took practice and I had not mastered it yet. And if I was really being honest with myself, at this point, I wasn't sure if I ever would.

I opened my mouth to change the subject, in case Jer didn't want to talk about it, but instantly stopped. Hadn't Izzy mentioned something about Jer's dad being high up in research here? What if he and Cy were arguing about Ralph?

As if confirming my worst fears, I watched Jer's dad shake his head before Cyrus straightened slightly and balled his right hand into a fist. His familiar eyes briefly made contact with mine. What I saw there almost broke me. He looked...resigned.

Cyrus was a fucking force, and I couldn't think of a time in all my life where he buckled quite like that. What the hell was going on? The hair along my arms stood up and I was getting some serious capital-E-evil vibes from Jer's dad all of a sudden.

It was just a look, a brief glance really, on Cy's face. But sometimes there were moments where you just *knew* something was wrong. And this was one of them.

Blood hummed through my veins until it suddenly felt like a clamp was tightening around my ribs. I looked up to see Ro and Izzy snapping their fingers in front of my face. Something was really wrong. I could feel it in my gut.

"What?" I asked, my voice cracking slightly, like my nerves were trying to fight their way out of my throat.

"What are your plans for tonight?" Izzy rested her chin on her hand, studying me with that all-knowing look of hers. How had she learned to read me so well, so quickly?

I shook my head and mentioned something about my team

ditching me for the day. When I turned back behind me, determined to insert myself into the conversation, Cyrus and Jer's dad were gone. Seamus was alone, absently running a hand through his hair, lost in his thoughts. There was belated frustration there on his face, like he was trying to put together a puzzle but didn't have all of the pieces he needed or even know how to go about looking for them.

Izzy flashed me a look of pity and set her fork down, temporarily ignoring her omelet. "Sorry, Max, that's shit."

"Six is moody, so it's not really a big shock," I said, glancing up at her and trying to focus back on the conversation. "What are you guys up to today?"

She looked down, picked up a piece of her toast and started ripping it into small crumbs. "We, uh, have a meeting with Seamus in a bit about a mission later tonight."

"That's awesome," I said. And I meant it. Ten minutes ago I would've been excited for her but also a touch envious. Now, I was just worried about Ralph. Something in my bones itched. I needed to do something.

"You should come with us," Jer said, straightening up, fiddling with his fingers. His ears turned a bit red as he cleared his throat. "Seriously, it should be a fun one and wouldn't be difficult for you to tag along."

There was an earnestness on his face that I hadn't seen before and I was struck by the thought that Jer might actually be developing a bit of crush on me. He'd been showing more and more interest since I'd arrived. And while Wade led me to believe he was just a huge flirt, maybe he wasn't. Or maybe in this case, he was flirting because he was legitimately interested in me.

I looked back at Seamus, resolve settling in my belly. If Cyrus wouldn't help me get Ralph out of the lab, then maybe Jer would. He clearly had some disagreements with his dad, but I'm sure he knew more than the rest of us about how to get one of the dungeon cells opened without causing too much of a stir. Thanks to the blueprints I found in the Six office, I had a working knowledge of the layout of the place.

Maybe Jer was the final piece I needed to make a clean escape for my hellhound.

"I'd like that," I said, lightly touching his hand as a coy grin stretched across my face. Or at least I hoped it looked coy and flirtatious. It wasn't really an expression I was familiar with. Since I didn't have a mirror in front of me, I wasn't sure how convincing I looked.

"Great," he said, a dimple indenting his cheek and genuine excitement shining in his eyes. "Meet us at our cabin at five. We aren't going far. We can brief you on the way."

"Yeah." Izzy's brow arched, her eyes narrowing as she studied me. She knew I wasn't into Jer in the way he seemed to hope. "I'll help you get ready."

Ro had been pretty silent since my arrival, but his posture was rod-straight and I could tell that he was focused on me with just as much curiosity.

My cheeks burned with guilt. I felt bad using Jer like this, but something told me Ralph didn't have any other options. And with the guys and Declan out for most of the night, I wouldn't have anyone keeping track of me later. It was the best chance I'd get for some freedom.

I looked from Ro to Izzy and nodded, a silent promise I'd fill them in on what was going through my head. We were getting Ralph out.

Tonight.

13
MAX

"So," I said, looking down at the outfit Izzy had instructed me to wear. "What kind of mission is this exactly?"

I was in skin-tight dark jeans with a dark green top that had a pretty hefty V carved into the neckline. Call me old fashioned, but I assumed a mission hunting supernatural creatures would involve some athletic wear and camouflage. Maybe even some walkie talkies.

We were packed together in one of the Guild SUVs and I was squashed in between Jer and Ro. Mavis and Sharla were meeting us in town a little later.

"People in town have been reporting wolf sightings," Jer said, his eyes moving from my chest to my face. Did guys really think that girls didn't realize when their attention was south of the eyes?

I pulled the top up an inch or two, trying not to get disheartened when it fell back down.

"Werewolves?" I asked, my stomach dropping. "This close to such a huge protector population? Again?" Werewolves were humanoids, so they were supposed to be pretty smart. This seemed like an irrational move. But I couldn't deny the fact that on some level, a part of me believed it to be true.

Those yellow eyes. I thought back to an earlier conversation with Ten. Hadn't they mentioned one of the recruits made a claim about a wolf on campus? Directly on our grounds? That meant this was the second reported sighting now. Not even counting whatever illusion I did or didn't see last night. Was it the same wolf or were there multiple?

Arnell shook his head, his eyes meeting mine in the rearview mirror as he drove our car down the road. "Probably nothing, to be honest. Regular wolves live in the area, and it's rare for werewolves to be cut off from a pack. Our people have intercepted some intel down at the sheriff station that hikers have reported sightings of a single, very large wolf deep in the woods." He shrugged, his dark eyes glancing briefly towards Ro on my right. "My best guess is that it's just that—a very large wolf. Probably won't see much action tonight, mostly just a Guild-sanctioned excuse for a night on the town. These are the easiest and often the most fun missions we are assigned. Days like tonight, our jobs are a cakewalk."

I shivered, thinking back to the wolf that attacked Michael a few weeks ago. It felt like it was a lifetime ago—like I was a completely different girl, living in that small cabin with Ro and Cyrus.

I thought about that moment, about the wolf pulling Michael into an alley, about the way that Ralph chased him or her off. There wasn't another wolf around, I was sure of it. Even in the adrenaline haze of that moment, I knew with a visceral certainty that it was a lone wolf, cut off from a pack. Maybe Guild intel was wrong. Maybe more wolves ran solo than we realized.

"They aren't always in packs," Ro said, his voice low. Apparently I wasn't the only one remembering that night that had set our path with the Guild in motion.

It was the first time he'd spoken since we'd left. I nudged his arm lightly with my shoulder, a silent check in to see if he was okay. He squeezed my hand softly in answer.

Yes, but thanks.

Arnell met my eyes again, tilting his head. I read the silent ask there—can you please figure out why your brother is being so short with me all of a sudden?

It was on my list of things to figure out, so I winked subtly. I was starting to get more and more concerned with Ro's standoffishness. He was always the more serious of the two of us, but lately, it seemed like he was taking that stoicism to another level entirely.

Did he hate it here? Was he missing home and our lives back on the outskirts of town, away from society and protector business? I leaned my head against him, hoping that for now, my presence would soothe whatever turmoil was going on behind his tense blue eyes.

Arnell's lip twitched in a forced small grin. "Well, it's a full moon tonight and while werewolves can transition into a wolf whenever they want, their instinct to do so is heightened when the moon is full. And it's the weekend, so the town will be full of people, a lot of them drunk with lowered inhibitions. Kind of a free for all for any creature that wants to go hunting."

"Don't werewolves usually just hunt random critters they find in the forest?" I asked, thinking back to everything I'd read about them.

"Yes," Jer said, his knee crowding into my space, "but if a werewolf really is this close to people, it's because it means to be. Even more so if it's this close to our Headquarters."

"And if there's an attack," Izzy said, finishing his thought, "it'll be tonight. But in the meantime, we get to have some fun people-watching in town and grabbing some food."

The rest of the short drive was quiet, all of us lost in our thoughts. I tried to shake my focus away from last night with Eli. If I really had seen a werewolf, it sounded like I'd for sure meet it again tonight.

Arnell found parking pretty quickly for a busy Sunday night. The storefronts and restaurant windows all emanated with a warm glow. Dozens of locals were walking around, shopping and grabbing a bite with their friends. I wondered how many of them were human.

"So," Izzy said, glancing towards the guys. They were walking ahead of us, debating where they wanted to stop for dinner. "Going to tell me what's going on or will I have to beat it out of you?"

"It's Ralph," I said, trying to keep my voice down low. I liked Ten a lot, but Cy made it clear that I wasn't to talk about Ralph or that night at Vanish with anyone who didn't need to know. And so far, outside of Ro and Six, Izzy was the only person I trusted completely with the details of that night. "The hellhound in the lab."

Izzy arched her perfectly-plucked brow and looked at me like I was completely dense. "Yeah, no shit, Sherlock. There's literally only one Ralph you'd be talking about."

"Well," I looked up at the guys, making sure they were still out of earshot, "I'm breaking him out. Tonight." I let out a long breath, hoping she wouldn't judge me too hard for the next part. "And I'm going to see if Jer can help me do it."

Her gray eyes lit up with a mischievous excitement and she grabbed my arm. "That makes so much sense now. Why didn't we think of using sex to get to Ralph sooner?"

"Not sex, just flirting," I corrected as I pulled at the hem of my shirt. "You won't say anything will you?"

"Hell no!" She stopped walking and crossed her arms. "You know I'm going with, right?"

I grinned. I didn't want her getting in trouble, but I'd take all the help I could get right now. I had a feeling Ralph wasn't going to be kept alive in the labs much longer. I couldn't prove it exactly, but I was certain I was right.

Sharla and the guys turned into a restaurant about a block up from us, and Jer waited at the door, a smile plastered to his face. "Let's go, we're starving. Pizza's on me tonight."

We jogged to catch up, shivers running down my spine when

I recognized the building. They'd walked into an Italian restaurant, but it was next door to Vanish. I tried to temper my fear and deliberately not rush by when we passed the alley. It seemed so unremarkable right now, filled with nothing but some lamps and dumpsters. How could I have almost died just a few feet away from where I now stood?

As if sensing my thoughts, Izzy grabbed my hands and winked before pulling me forward. "Come on, dude. I've got your back. Let's focus on Mission: Hellhound for now."

After stuffing our faces with pizza and pasta, we were leisurely patrolling the streets. I waited until the rest of Ten was ahead before filling Ro in on the plan. He was more difficult to persuade than Izzy, but I knew he'd help no matter what.

I watched him as he studied Arnell, something he only allowed himself to do when he thought no one was looking.

"So," I said, tugging softly on his shirt.

"So, what?" Ro nudged my hand away and kicked a stray rock towards the street.

"So," I said again, frustrated, "want to tell me what the hell is going on with Arnell?"

"I don't know what you're talking about." He was avoiding eye contact, which we both knew meant he was lying. Ro was great at many things, but fortunately lying to me was not one of them.

"Well," Izzy said, coming to my aid, "You guys seemed pretty interested in each other when you first got here."

"And things got awkward at some point. So spill," I said, genuinely concerned. I liked Arnell. And I loved Ro. And more than anything in the world, I wanted Ro to be happy.

"It's nothing, Max, just drop it, okay? I'll help you with the Ralph thing, let's focus on that. Arnell doesn't matter."

While we needed to stay focused, I wasn't letting it go that easily. Especially not when it was becoming alarmingly clear that Ro was legitimately distressed by the whole thing.

"Did something happen?" I glanced at Arnell. "Did he do

something to you or something? I can fight him if you want? You just say when and where."

Ro tried to suppress a grin, but I saw the curve forming at the corner of his mouth despite his efforts. "No. He didn't do anything to me. I just want to stay focused. Arnell is a distraction. I don't need that right now."

"Nope, nope, hold up," Izzy said, stopping cold. "We're protectors. Our lives are, by definition, dangerous and complicated. That does not mean you don't get to enjoy your life whenever possible. Arnell is hot as hell. You're hot as hell." She held her hands apart before clapping them loudly together. "Be hot as hell together."

Ro laughed, a soft rumbly sound that I hadn't heard in far longer than I realized. Then, all at once, the mirth died on his face.

"Tell me," I said, studying him.

"You can't just let this go?" he asked, a frown line creasing the normally smooth skin between his brows.

I rubbed the line away, trying to literally erase the tension. "I won't let this go."

"The night you were attacked. I was focusing on Arnell, on having fun, on flirting."

"Yeah, so?" I prompted.

Ro let out a long sigh and it was like I could feel the fear enveloping him. "Jesus, Max. You almost died. You do get that, right?"

"What does that have to do with anything? I didn't. I'm still here, still alive."

"Oh," Izzy said, clearly able to follow something I couldn't. "You think that Max wouldn't have been attacked if you were there with her. And so now," she said, waving her hand as if guiding me through the tangled weave of her thoughts, "you think you'll be a better protector and brother if you just completely don't have a life and live for nothing but the hunt and watching her back?"

Ro's eyes narrowed at the condescension in her voice. "It's not like that."

"So what's it like then?" I asked, guilt streaming through my body in cold waves. Was I really the reason that Ro was letting go of something good? He'd grown up with so little—and now that he had the opportunity for something big, for something more, he was letting it pass by because of me?

He paused for a moment, as we walked, thinking. "Okay, so it is like that. It doesn't matter though, we're protectors. I'm allowed to focus on my job. I'm encouraged to, even."

I stopped, waiting the thirty seconds it took for Ro to follow suit. "Hell no." I tried to pull the anger from my tone, but hopefully Ro knew it was coming from a place of love. "You don't get to make that choice. You don't get to be all puppy-dog-eyed brokenhearted because of me. I won't be your excuse for that. That's a cruel burden to bear. I want you to be happy. What happened to me was not your fault." I paused, took a big breath before grabbing his chin and forcing his eyes to meet mine directly. "It. Was. Not. Your. Fault. And I'm alive, you big doofus. I may be smaller than the average protector, but I am also pretty badass, in case you haven't noticed. Do you understand that? Because I need you to understand."

I waited, counting the seconds until Ro finally nodded, resolve settling across his features. "I understand."

"Good," I said, grinning. "I'm okay Ro, I didn't die that night." I pulled him into a hug. Ro wasn't the most affectionate person, but he breathed out a choked sigh and collapsed his weight into me, his fingers digging into my shoulders as he squeezed. I'd been so concerned about my own shit that I didn't realize how much that night with the vamp had affected him.

"I think we should split up, newbie and a member of Ten, so we can cover more ground," Mavis said, glancing back at us. "Izzy, do you want to come with me and Sharla?"

With a wink directed towards me and Ro, she bounced away, brimming with excitement. I think we were both stoked to be on our first real mission, even if Ten didn't know anything about the mission we were really focusing on. But as far as we were concerned, Mission: Hellhound was officially a go.

I nudged Ro with my elbow, a not-so-gentle encouragement for him to speak up.

He rolled his head from side to side, like he was preparing for a battle and walked up to Arnell. "Cool if I go with you?"

Arnell's face broke out into that million-dollar smile I'd grown so fond of and my stomach swooped with happiness. I really liked Arnell, and Ro deserved all of the happiness in the world. More, even. And I refused to be an obstacle in the way of him achieving it.

"That leaves you and me then, Max," Jer said, heading in my direction. There was a shyness about him tonight that I wasn't used to. He was almost completely silent during our meal.

I threaded my arm through his, locking our elbows together. I gave myself a quick pep talk about using my charm to save Ralph as we walked away from the rest of the group. Hopefully if there was a wolf around, we'd find it between all of us.

We both walked in an awkward silence for a few minutes, studying the various people throughout the town. They all looked so happy, so blissfully unaware of all the monsters living in the shadows.

"Are most of the people who live here humans?" I asked, kicking a rock along the street as we walked. Everyone out tonight seemed so carefree and happy, I couldn't imagine them throwing themselves into battle on the daily.

Jer nodded, the red in his hair catching in the streetlamps. "Yeah, for the most part. There are quite a few retired protectors who live in this part of town, as well as some who have non-Guild-based jobs. But for the most part, it's just a quaint little town close to us with quite a bit of Guild money flowing through it."

Seeing an opportunity, I looked up at him. "Did you grow up around here?"

"Yeah, I've been in this area most of my life. My dad was stationed at one of the smaller satellites for a while, but he's been at the North American Guild now for about ten years."

My stomach kicked at the mention of his dad and I silently congratulated myself for getting our conversation on track so quickly. "I got the feeling earlier that you and your dad don't get along too well."

"Yeah, you could definitely say that." He blew out a heavy breath and gave my arm a little squeeze. "Protector families can always be a little volatile and competitive. Usually kids get groomed for research careers pretty early. I never really took too well to my chemistry and biology classes, so when it became pretty obvious that wasn't going to be the path for me, things grew strained between us. My dad considers the field teams to be full of mindless brutes, so I think he was really disappointed when he realized that was the path I wanted to go down."

I frowned, trying to imagine the tension. Cyrus wasn't exactly warm and fuzzy, but I knew at the end of the day he just wanted me to be happy and safe.

"I'm sorry," I said, meaning it. "That's really rough. And a lot of pressure to put on a kid."

"It is, but we know where we stand now and I really love my team. It's where I'm supposed to be. Dad's just extra sore about it the last couple years because my mom died fighting a vampire. I think on some level, he's worried I'll suffer the same fate and it's easier for him to just create distance between us now. You know, the whole 'don't set any unrealistic expectations, just to get disappointed down the line' approach to life."

I squeezed Jer's hand while I watched the pain draw shadows across his face. He put on such a tough, flirty, and carefree persona most of the time, it felt like I was really meeting him for the first time since arriving here. How many protectors felt the need to do this—to hide behind bravado and a sly grin?

I took a breath, steadying myself. Guilt was keeping me quieter than I should've been. Ralph's miserable expression the last time I was in the lab fell through my thoughts and I straightened, ready to do what I needed to do. I silently promised myself that if he didn't hate me tomorrow for using him to get into the lab, I'd go out on a real date with Jer in the future. Eli made it abundantly clear last night that he wasn't interested. And maybe Jer deserved a shot. Maybe he was a nice guy under all the fake ego and flirty reputation.

"Do you know much about your dad's work?" I asked, toying with the hem of my top as we passed a drunk couple meandering down the street while they window shopped.

"He tells me a little here and there." He grinned, looking down at me. "I think he's still secretly hoping I'll switch career paths eventually. Like I'll wake up one day with a penchant for test tubes and experiments or something."

The mention of experiments made me shiver. "Have you been down there—you know, seen any of the creatures they experiment on?"

A fond expression crossed his face and it was like he'd disappeared for a moment, lost in a distant memory. "I used to sneak down there quite a bit as a kid to study whichever vamp or wolf they were experimenting on. And then, maybe three or four years ago, when my dad really pissed me off, I'd made plans to free one of them that I'd grown attached to." He shook his head, embarrassed. "It was the year after my mom died and I think I just wanted out of the protector life. Wanted to destroy some part of it. See one of the creatures in action. It was seriously misguided."

My adrenaline spiked and I hoped that my heartbeat wasn't pounding as loudly as it sounded to me. "And did you?" I pressed.

He shook his head. "No, I chickened out at the last minute. They brought a protector in who was beaten to a pulp by a vampire, and I just couldn't let one of them loose after that. It all sort of sunk in then—what happened to my mom—and gave me my purpose back."

I could understand that. Being up close and personal with a

vamp, and then seeing Wade after the attack—my focus on being the best protector I could be was much more solidified now. But I could see how easy it would be to soften towards one, why Jer might be tempted. I hadn't been afraid of the little girl until she started pulling against her restraints to drain me like a milkshake. The lab and those cells were important, I understood that now.

But Ralph wasn't a vampire. He was good. I knew he was. And I also knew that he did not belong down there.

"I don't know," I said, twirling my hair a little in what I hoped was a sort of seductive way, all the while hating myself intensely for having to manipulate Jer for the information I needed. "It sounds like your dad maybe underestimated you. I think it takes more than a brute to break into a top secret lab all the time. And you have to be pretty smart if you came up with a plan to let one of those beasts free in the first place. I doubt most protectors in The Guild could do that." I leaned into his side a bit and prayed that I wasn't laying it on too thick.

Jer's eyes crinkled a bit as he looked down at me, a genuine smile pulling up the corners of his lips—a smile that made guilt pool deep in my belly. "It wasn't all that impressive. The individual cells themselves are impenetrable, but if you swipe one of the higher up's cards, you can get into the main lab where the backdoors to the cells are."

"That's it?" I asked, putting as much confusion into my tone as possible. "I would think protectors had more failsafes than that."

"They do," he continued, "but not against protectors. Once you're in the main room, you need a drop of a higher-up protector's blood to open the individual door. It blocks whatever magic they use to keep the beasts contained." He shrugged, grin widening. "Since my dad is one of the top guys down there, he has clearance and his blood works. And my protector line comes from him, so…"

"So your blood would have opened it," I finished, my head

rushing with excitement. Would Jer give me his blood if I asked for it? I blanched at the thought. There was no way I could just casually be like *hey, babe, can I steal some of that O-neg you're rocking?* I was lost in thought when I went barrelling into something. No, someone.

"Thought I gave explicit directions to be home by nightfall?" Declan's emerald eyes were sparkling down at me and I watched as they moved over to Jer and down to the spot where our hands were linked.

So it was her messy scrawl that left the note?

"You guys aren't in charge of my curfew," I said, my cheeks reddening with the thought of the last time she'd snuck up on me and caught me doing something I wasn't supposed to be doing. "You ditched me for the day, so Ten let me tag along."

"Oh, don't be like that, Max," Eli said as he hopped out of a bright red car next to us. "They sort of just sprung you on us, we weren't prepared to have you along today." He circled the car and paused. "Although it doesn't exactly look like you're on official Ten business right now, either," he added, his thick eyebrows arched in challenge. He put his arm around my shoulders and pulled me to his side, away from Jer. "We'll take her from here, Jer. Get back to whatever mission you're on."

"Don't be such a prick, Eli," Jer said, the open expression he'd had with me suddenly walling back up into the mask he donned most days. Protectors were an emotionally constipated bunch. "Let her finish the mission tonight and then tomor—" He cut off instantly, his stance stiffening. "Holy shit."

I followed Jer's line of sight to the opening in the woods a few feet away from us.

And then I saw it: a large wolf baring its teeth at us.

Familiar yellow eyes glaring right into mine.

14
MAX

Without a second thought, I reached into the thigh holster I'd fixed to the outside of my jeans and grabbed my silver-coated knife. Before I could take off to attack the wolf, Declan and Eli positioned themselves in front of me. While it was sweet they wanted to protect me, I guess, I was frustrated I was being blocked from the action. Adrenaline coursed through my veins and I pushed through the gap between them to get a better look at the wolf. My gaze was met with dark brown fur and familiar yellow eyes. Either all werewolves looked identical, or this was the exact one that had attacked me before.

The exact one I'd seen last night out at the pond.

"You," I said, trying to elbow Dec and Eli to the side so that I could get after Wolfie. This asshole ruined my one and only date. And then whatever last night with Eli was.

The beast was as large as I remembered and giant, sharp teeth were bared in the shadow of a vicious growl. Its eyes were fixed on Jer, and a heated, visceral tension filled the air. The sound emanating from the wolf was so low that I could feel the environment grow heavy with it.

As if suddenly aware that I was digging my limbs into her, Declan looked down at me. Her sharp eyes were filled with confusion, but also a healthy dose of fear—but the fear seemed directed towards me, not the wolf. In fact, she was presenting her back to the wolf, which didn't make any sense.

Who turned their back on an enemy? Especially one as vicious as a werewolf.

"You should go," Declan said, looking from me to Jer. "Eli and I can handle this from here. Jer, take her home."

Jer rolled his eyes before shoulder-checking Declan out of the way. "Why are the members of your team all such fucking glory hogs?" He lunged towards the wolf, right arm pulled back and ready to strike.

My breath caught in my throat as I watched Jer land on top of the creature, the two of them a pile of limbs and muscles in alternating layers of fur and skin.

"Fuck," Eli said, running towards them. "What a fucking mess."

He ripped Jer away from the wolf just as the creature's jaws would have clamped around his neck. The thick black hilt of Jer's blade was protruding from the wolf's left side. It was enough to cause some heavy damage that the creature would need to heal from, but not enough to kill it. Not even close.

Eli and the wolf squared off, studying each other. There was a stillness to their staredown that didn't make sense and I held my breath waiting for one of them to lunge. In a bizarrely human gesture, the beast nodded ever so slightly a second before Eli pounced. By the time Eli's knife met the spot where the wolf was standing, it was gone; I watched, shocked, as the wolf went barrelling back into the forest.

I lunged to chase after it, but Declan caught my momentum just in time, wrapping her lean arms around my waist. I fell against her chest with a thud as she held me to her, her heart beating a quick pattern into my spine. She radiated calm, collected energy, but it was clear she was flustered, afraid.

I stopped fighting against her grip until we were locked like that, in an odd hug. As if realizing that she was still holding me to her, Declan's arm fell. She took a step away from me, my back suddenly struck with the chill air of the night.

"What the hell, Eli," Jer said. He lifted himself back onto his two feet and I noticed a soft trickle of blood dripping from his mouth. "I would've had him. You let him get away."

Declan shared a look with Eli before glancing over at Jer, her lip curled in frustration, like she was chastising a child. "Shut the hell up, Jer. Eli saved your ass. You'd be wolf meat if he hadn't grabbed you. And the wolf would be dead if you hadn't gone charging at it like a bloody asshole."

Jer's nostrils flared with a heat I hadn't seen before. His usual cocky persona was gone, as was the vulnerable Jer I'd spent most of the evening with. "Fuck off, both of you, I'm going after it."

"You're going back home," Declan said, her voice low and filled with a menacing warning.

Atlas was definitely the leader of the group, but Declan held a controlled, immeasurable power. And it was a power that grew more and more clear the longer I observed her.

She was a bit of an outlier on campus and didn't seem to have many—or any—friends outside of her team. Even so, in my time at The Guild, I'd seen that people didn't challenge her—didn't cross her. She was the smallest on Six, that much was clear, but she wasn't a pushover and I could see Jer wilting under her glare like a pruned flower.

The hair on my arms was standing on end from the energy and I looked back as Izzy, Ro, and the rest of Ten made their way over to us, confusion mirrored on all of their faces.

"We should go after it," I said, watching as the group caught up to us. "There's way more of us. The wolf doesn't stand a chance."

Eli walked up to me and touched my chin, tilting it to one side and then the other as if convinced I was harmed in some way. Apparently satisfied, he dropped his hand from my face and ran it through his hair in frustration. "Atlas is in the woods, he'll take care of it. Everyone else should head back."

"Everything okay?" Izzy asked, her eyebrow arched at the energy brimming around the group. "We heard a commotion and —" she glanced at Jer and walked over to him. "Shit, you're bleeding. Were you hurt? Bit?"

Jer shook his head, but didn't offer anything more. He was practically vibrating with frustration and I watched, annoyed, as he stared Eli and Declan down with an I'll-kill-you-later glare.

Fucking testosterone. Thank the gods that Ro didn't put me through that shit—proving that men were capable of being reasonable and composed on occasion.

"We shouldn't leave Atlas out there alone though," I said, concern clouding my thoughts. One protector against a werewolf wasn't a desirable ratio.

"He's not alone," Declan said, interrupting me before I could get another argument in edgewise. "There's another team with him. They'll be more than capable of handling it." She spun her glare on me, stepping closer and it took everything in me to not wilt like Jer had.

"This is pointless." Jer's jaw tightened and he eyed the non-existent space between me and Declan. "I'll take you home, Max."

Before he could walk more than two steps towards me, Eli shook his head. "We've got her." There was an edge to the words and I glanced at Izzy with a question in my eyes. What the hell was going on between Jer and Team Six. The confusion on her face made it clear she was just as clueless. I hadn't seen any of the teams work together really, and the competition between them was startling. I wondered who Atlas was working with now, and why Six didn't have that sort of relationship with Ten.

"Jer brought me, he can take me home," I said, though I wasn't exactly dying to be in a car with Jer and his attitude right now. At least Izzy and Ro would be there too. I hadn't forgotten the fact that while the guys had ditched me today when I was supposed to be shadowing them, Ten had let me into their circle with open arms. My loyalty was with them.

Plus hanging out with Ten didn't spike my emotions in a million different directions. Being around Six sometimes felt like hanging out with and befriending a hurricane.

"Don't be stubborn, Max," Eli said. Exhaustion colored his features and I almost felt sorry for him. He couldn't quite meet my eyes when he spoke and shame curdled in my belly. Was he disgusted by our kiss last night? He exhaled and glanced around the street filled with unsuspecting barhoppers like he was surveying it for something.

"Besides," Declan added, slow and drawn-out-like, as she studied Eli with curiosity, "Wade is awake. They're taking him back to the cabin now and we should be there when he arrives."

I wasn't sure who 'they' was, but I didn't really care.

Awake. Wade was awake. Relief fluttered through my body and I suddenly felt lighter than I had in weeks. I knew he'd wake up, somehow I was sure of it. But now that I was faced with the truth of that belief, I realized how fragile that hope really was. My skin was buzzing with excitement and I almost jumped towards Declan to give her a hug.

Almost. It was going to be a long night.

Turning, I stepped up to Jer and tore a piece of fabric from my top, the thin material ripping like paper. "You're bleeding."

I swiped the blood from his mouth in a smooth stroke. My fingers lingered briefly on his bottom lip, drawing a small gasp from him. I could feel Eli's eyes boring into my back, and I couldn't help but feel a bit satisfied that he was seeing this, petty as it was.

But I didn't linger. I wanted to get back to Wade as soon as possible. Excitement was rushing through my blood at the thought of seeing him awake again.

With a quick hug, I moved away from Jer, ready to follow Eli and Declan back to the cabin. The drive and walk back was filled with silence, the only acknowledgement that I was there filtered through occasional heavy glances.

They were doing that thing again, where they communicated with nothing but eyes and perfectly timed sighs, and I was big enough to admit that I wanted in on that conversation something furious. But more than ever, it was clear that I was on the outside of their little family and, more than that, I understood. They'd been together for years, protected each other, cared for each other. I was an intruder, throwing all of their plans and goals for a wickedly unexpected loop. They hadn't asked that I apprentice with them, that I move in with them and disrupt their living space.

But understanding didn't completely eek out my jealousy, my annoying desire to be a part of what they had.

When we reached the cabin, a warm glow from the kitchen window lit up the lines of trees, casting interesting shadows along the grass and walking path.

"I'm fine, seriously. You can leave. They'll be here soon, I'm sure." Wade's grumbled voice echoed down the hall when we entered the cabin. Three protectors I'd never seen before walked towards us and the door. Their faces were all so stoic that they almost looked identical. One gave a single nod to Declan before leading the other two out the door.

"Seriously, please go," Wade said. He must've mistaken our footsteps for the surly dudes.

With a quick grin, I went tearing off upstairs until I came to the only room in the hall with the lights on. I knocked once, not even waiting for an answer to open the door.

"Jesus, did you have to—" Wade's face lit up with a giant smile when he saw me. "Max? What are you doing here?"

Forgetting decorum, I ran towards the bed and grabbed him into a hug. A warm feeling settled in my belly, and for the first time in days, I could breathe out fully. The lightness that was left over when my worry disintegrated clued me in to how concerned I'd really been. When had Wade whittled his way into my mind so completely?

"I live here now. It's sort of a long story. What happened? Do they know why you were unconscious? You're okay?"

Wade made some grumbling noises and I realized that I had smashed his face into my chest out of excitement. I stepped back, embarrassed, catching a mirrored flush on his cheeks.

With a cheeky, wistful grin he nodded. "I'm fine. Woke up a few hours ago. They ran a bunch of tests, and now—well, now I'm here."

I was vaguely aware of Declan and Eli filing into the room behind me.

"Good to have you back, man," Eli said, genuine warmth lighting up his eyes as the strained tension between us melted off his face.

Declan nodded, moving around to the other side of the bed and patting Wade on the shoulder. "Seconded. And," she added, shooting a brief glance at me, "maybe now that you're here, you can keep Max in line."

"What happened to you, Wade?" I asked, curiosity taking over now that I was convinced he was alive and okay. I wasn't going to give Declan the satisfaction of responding to her comment.

His eyes went hazy, briefly, like he was trying to physically sort through his memories but they kept slipping out of reach. With a sigh, he shook his head. "Honestly, I don't remember. The fight, everything, it's all sort of a blur."

"Nothing's come back to you then?" Declan leaned against the wall, her shirt pulling up a bit at the hem. I looked away from the patch of smooth, cream skin above her jeans, embarrassment clouding my eyes.

"Nothing. I remember taking down one wolf, but that was it." Wade reached over to his left and grabbed a glass of water on his bedside table. It was only after his arm brushed mine that I realized I was sitting on his bed, dangerously close to a very shirtless Wade. Blushing, I braced myself to stand up, but Wade's other hand came over and clasped mine, keeping me there.

"You took down a wolf by yourself?" It took every fiber of my being to focus on his words, and not on the feel of his rough, calloused fingers against my own.

No one had filled me in on any of the details about that night, other than Atlas's tepid confession that both wolves and vamps had been present.

"He took down several," Eli said, and there was a guardedness about him suddenly. He couldn't quite bring himself to look Wade in the eyes. A day ago, I wouldn't have recognized it, but something about Eli's vulnerability and sadness reminded me so much of Ro's. Did he blame himself for not being there? For not fighting off the monsters alongside his brother?

As if reading my mind, Wade dropped my hand and playfully punched Eli. Well, he tried anyway, but Eli was standing a bit too far away, like he didn't want to encroach on the moment so he lingered on the periphery. "Dude, it was senseless of me. I went in solo and I shouldn't have. If I hadn't, maybe we would've taken them all down and we would have had more intel."

Eli opened his mouth, but I stood, shaking my head. "Nope, no more pity party. Wade's okay. Everyone's alive. That's what matters. Everything else is a learning experience."

"Okay, Yoda," Declan said. Her mouth lifting slightly at the corners as she stared at me with a level of focus that had me squirming.

"Right, well, I'm sure Atlas will be home soon. I'll leave you guys to catch up. Let me know if you need anything." I kissed Wade's cheek, trying to ignore the dizzying dance in my stomach, and then left them for my room. I'd wait a few hours, give them every certainty that I was fast asleep. And then—well, then I'd use every stealth bone in my body to go sneak Ralph out.

Now that Wade was okay, my mind was completely free to focus on rescuing my hellhound.

I CRACKED OPEN MY WINDOW AND CRAWLED OUT, INSTEAD OF risking exposure by trying to tiptoe through the cabin. A sharp thrill ran through me as I looked at my bed, stuffed with pillows in a vaguely humanesque shape. It was a tactic that seemed to work well enough on TV, so hopefully it'd work for me if Declan or one of the boys came sneaking into my room in the middle of the night. But really, if the guys were going to sneak into my room while I was asleep, I had bigger concerns than getting busted on my prison break mission.

With one last deep breath in, I pushed off from my window and landed softly on the grass. Since my room was only on the second floor, it wasn't too difficult to stick the landing without rolling my ankle. While I felt a sharp stab of guilt for not taking Izzy and Ro with me, I wasn't sure I could reach them without waking up everyone in Ten. We'd been separated so quickly after the mission in town that we didn't have time to make any concrete plans. So I was tackling the rescue mission solo, resigned to ask them for forgiveness rather than permission.

Surprisingly, the grounds themselves were quiet. Using the edge of the forest for cover, I made my way to The Guild's main campus, with buildings connected by various halls and bridges like a complex, winding maze.

Without too much fuss, I made it to the now-familiar research grounds, thankful once again for Greta's keycard. It was now a permanent fixture in my wardrobe, currently placed discreetly against the inner rim of my leggings. Other than Izzy, she was by far the best friend I'd made since joining The Guild.

I owed the woman an enormous box of chocolates for saving my ass so many times.

My mind had been shuffling through possible outcomes for Ralph all night, and it took every ounce of willpower I had not to break out into an all-out run. Hopefully when I found him, I wouldn't have trouble leading him out of the grounds unnoticed.

While I still got lost regularly, I had a feeling that Ralph's nose could lead us to the safety of campus lines when we needed it.

Rounding the final corner, I hurried to Ralph's hallway, praising my good luck for not encountering any guards or protectors on my route.

Until I came up to Ralph's empty cell.

The sound of my blood rushing through my veins pulsed in my ears and tears pricked the corners of my eyes. Was I too late? What had they done with him? Where had they taken him?

I knew in my gut that something was going down with Ralph tonight, but I thought I'd been quick enough. Maybe I shouldn't have gone back with Eli and Dec? If I had resisted, gone home with Izzy and Ro instead of rushing back to see Wade— then I wouldn't have had to wait until the house was silent to sneak out.

"They took him."

I whipped around, coming face-to-face with the golden vampire; his mismatched eyes glittered with amusement.

"Wh-what? Where?" It was all I could manage to push out, my tongue was so dry I was shocked any whisper at all made it past my lips.

The vampire tilted his head as I walked a few steps towards him. He studied me with open curiosity and amusement.

"Please." The word was forceful, angry. I squared my shoulders, no longer willing to play the mouse in this game of his.

"I could tell you," he said, ambivalence painted across his stark features. He seemed to be wrestling with himself, but I knew when he'd reached a decision. His pale face broke into a terrifying grin as he walked another step towards the glass so that all that separated us was an invisible wall. "But I think I'll show you instead."

"Show me?" I echoed back. "Show me what?"

"I heard the guards speaking. They're running some final tests on your hound." He shrugged, lazy and languid. "And then they will kill him. Let me out, and I'll take you to where they're keeping him."

15

DARIUS

The girl with the long brown hair and perpetually sultry eyes, Max as they called her, looked at me like I was Medusa. Her entire body was tensed, like she expected me to jump through the barrier and devour her. Truth be told, she was probably right.

Her pulse was beating so hard, I could see it pumping against the smooth skin of her neck. I narrowed my eyes, studying the spot. I reminded myself that she had been tasted before. Whoever was in charge of her protection was clearly incompetent. Most protectors were.

The moments passed while she decided, and up until she breathed out one low, exasperated breath, I was convinced she wouldn't take me up on my offer.

"Fine," she said, the word mumbled so low that my heightened hearing could barely even pick it up. "But if you kill me, I'm coming back from the dead, Dracula-style, and fucking castrating you."

My lips pulled back until I found myself doing that thing again—that thing that seemed to only happen when the little protector was in my vicinity.

Smiling.

And what an odd thing to smile about, castration.

I didn't think she could really get me out of here, but the thought of her attempting it was entertainment enough to keep me occupied for days. By then, of course, her beloved hellhound would be dead. But the odds of us saving the beast even if she did manage to get me out were nonexistent anyway.

The creature's death warrant was signed as soon as it crossed the threshold. And if the creature did escape, he would be hunted down again. And again. And again. Until he was buried six feet under after they got whatever it was they wanted out of him. She was naive if she ever thought otherwise.

Looking at her now though, at her large, inquisitive eyes, at the glow that seemed to highlight her skin like she was painstakingly painted by an artist—her naivety shone through in droves.

I leaned against the unbreakable glass, disappointment flaring through me when she shot me a resigned glance and then disappeared from my sight. I'd expected the game to be more entertaining than that, to unfold before my eyes. I was looking forward to at least an hour of her failed attempts, throwing things pointlessly against the window until she inevitably alerted some guards.

Of course if that happened, she would be barred from visiting me again. How she got down here as frequently as she did was a marvel. Then again, if the hellhound was dead, she would have no reason to visit at all. The thought made my skin itch, uncomfortable and tight.

My head whipped around so quickly that I was shocked to find it still attached to my neck. I heard the recognizable beeping that came just before someone opened my glorified prison. I counted the seconds, but no gas released from the ceiling as it usually did. In all of my years here, I'd never been conscious when the door to my cell was opened. Had she managed it already?

Perhaps she stole the codes, or whatever was used to gain entry, from some unsuspecting, inadequate guard. It would be enough though, wouldn't get her all the way through. Not without the bloo—

All at once she was standing before me, tucking a ragged scrap of green fabric into her hem. My senses were filled with her—a heady mix of juniper and the ocean. The scent was intoxicating. It'd been years since I'd been near the ocean. And her shampoo—vanilla? My feet lifted, one and then the other as I drew closer.

"How did you—" I shook my head, trying to dispel the shock coursing through my body.

"I, er, borrowed some blood," she said, lifting her arm between us as if her twig of a limb could stop me from closing the distance If I wanted to.

The small blade tucked into her fist was so miniscule I bit back a smile. "If I wanted you dead, little protector, that blade wouldn't stop me. You would, quite simply, just be dead."

She gulped, and I found myself studying her throat again, mesmerized by the movement. It'd been years since I tasted a human, even more since I tasted a protector. Something about her told me that she would be divine.

"Don't even think about it," she said, fear coating her words despite the determination in her eyes. And such remarkable eyes they were. Why wasn't I attacking her again? I wanted to drain her, yes, but why didn't I? "Take me to Ralph."

My face stretched—there was that smile again. What kind of naive oddball named a hellhound Ralph? If I hadn't seen the beast's appreciation of the name myself, I wouldn't have believed it. Of course, I knew well enough that hellhounds didn't understand or respond to human languages, but it was amusing to watch her think otherwise.

What was it about this girl that drew us beasts from hell to her? Her blood called to me, sure, but so did everything else.

"A deal is a deal," I said, spreading my arms in surrender. "I don't go back on my word. I'll take you to your hound. Or at least to my best guess at where he will be found."

She was surprised by my words, but so was I. I meant them. I would take her to her beast, I wanted to witness how this would all play out for myself. After years of dreaming of escape, it was finally here—and for the first time, surprisingly, running wasn't the first thing on my mind.

Unable to stop myself, I reached my fingers to the nape of her neck, satisfied by the small tremor that shook her body. Was she afraid? Or was it something else? Was she as drawn to me as I was to her?

Turning from her before I did something careless, like break my new toy before I even had a chance to appreciate it, I walked down the hall. I'd spent so much time chained up in various rooms that I had a decent understanding of the layout of the place—and I had an extensive-enough network built up amongst the other captives that I knew where they took creatures to be put down.

She followed, unwilling to get too close to me, but never more than a few steps behind. Her knife never wavered from the tight grip of her right hand, almost like it was a built-in security blanket, an extension of her hand.

Odd girl.

We continued in silence, winding through the halls in comfortable companionship. I was comfortable anyway. Judging from the racing dance of her heart, she was far from it. She looked around every corner we passed, but I'd be able to hear footsteps long before she could, and I felt her confidence gradually grow in my movements. It wasn't until we reached our destination that we ran into one of the lab coats.

Snivelling Rat, as I'd dubbed him, was perched above the hellhound—Ralph—injecting various concoctions into the creature's veins.

"No!" The girl went striding into the room, forgetting her fear of me and pulled Rat away. "What the hell are you doing to him? You're hurting him."

"What the hell are you doing here, girl? This one's slated to be put down." He shoved her to the ground, and I found a low, steady growl building in my throat. His beady, black eyes found mine, and terror filled his features. "Holy shit. D-d-did you let him out? What the fuck were you thinking? You don't understand, he's—"

I broke his neck, smiling as his body fell to the ground in a puddle of limbs and lard. "Sorry, Snivelly, we don't have time for a chat today."

The girl looked at me with horror shining in her eyes as she pressed a trembling finger to the lab rat's neck. She wouldn't find a pulse. "What did you do?"

I cracked my neck from side to side before dropping down to the dead man. With practiced fingers, I found a major artery and pierced his skin. I watched her as I pulled long, steady mouthfuls from the corpse. I shrugged as I finished my meal. "What? No sense wasting a meal."

Her normally brown skin paled, her forehead clammy with sweat as she shuffled away from me. "What have I done?"

I rolled my eyes. Protectors were always so dramatic. They killed my kind daily. What did it matter if one of their worst was gone? "Look, if it makes you feel better, he was a shit person. And I solemnly promise not to eat anyone else until I'm out of here."

I held up three fingers before her face to solidify my oath. Maybe if I looked less like a vampire and more like a boy scout, it would calm her nerves some.

Confusion marred her features and, as if she no longer had the capacity to acknowledge the situation, she turned to the hellhound. The creature's breathing was heavy and labored. Not good.

"What's wrong with him?" Her eyes glazed over with tears as she draped herself on top of the beast, searching for its pulse.

As if of its own accord, my hand reached forward to comfort her. I caught myself in time, and drew back. "I think we're too late."

Honestly, what did she expect? Protectors were ruthless. It was a shock the beast had lasted this long, with all of the tests they ran it through. He was strong as hell, but that wasn't enough to survive a place like this for long.

Tears spilled silently from her eyes now, puddling on the beast's face. There were worse ways to go, I guess, than a beautiful girl weeping over you. Lucky hound.

Her back was to me, and I was struck once again by the girl's carelessness. What kind of protector turned their back on a vampire? Especially after watching that vampire take down one of her kind?

We'd been here too long, someone would be by to make their next rounds any second. It was time for me to go. Committing her features to memory, I readied myself to leave. I'd keep my promise and not drain her dry, as tempting as it was, and as poetic as it would be—leaving her body alongside her pet's.

As I turned, I caught the eye of the hellhound. It seemed as if its breathing was normalizing, ever so slightly—far too small a change for a protector to notice. Curious.

Without a word, I grabbed a scalpel from the counter, and grabbed the girl's wrist. Without waiting for her to react, I sliced a long, thin incision. It was deep enough to encourage quick blood flow, not so deep she wouldn't heal from it within a minute or two. I watched as the blood spilled onto the hound's face, more than enough making its way between the creature's parted lips.

My nostrils flared as I breathed in her scent—she was overwhelming. It took everything I had not to sink my teeth into her neck, to feel the rush of her blood over my tongue. My eyes blurred just from the thought.

Her dark eyes filled with fear and determination. I pulled away just before her blade reached my neck, another annoying smile spreading across my face.

"What the hell are you doing?" Her eyes were wild. "Jesus,

Max. He's a vampire. Of course he's going to fucking attack you. What the hell were you thinking?"

She was talking to herself now, and something in me warmed at the thought. Such an odd girl.

I shot her a wide-eyed look and pointed down to her beast. The creature was standing now, acting as a barrier between me and the girl. Its lips were pulled back, a menacing noise emanating from his chest. I wasn't ignorant enough to goad a hellhound, so I stepped back, my hands raised in surrender.

"You're welcome," I said, bracing my shoeless feet on the linoleum, in case I needed to run for my life. "Could you call him down, please? Death-by-hellhound is a really undesirable way to die."

She ignored me. Her fear, anger, and grief seemed to evaporate in an instant as she threw herself onto her hound, all but forgetting my presence.

"How?" Her face was buried into the creature's fur, and I pushed down the unwelcome jealousy stirring my gut. I needed to leave this place—these protectors had addled my mind enough through the years.

"It's bound to you," I said, cocking my head to the side and listening to distant echoes. "It was a hunch." I reached down and grabbed her hand, cringing as the hound snapped at me. "I'm not going to hurt her, you ungrateful brute. But we need to go. At least three more protectors are coming. So unless you want to stand by and watch me have another feast—which, to be clear, I'm more than willing to indulge—we need to leave. Now."

Indecision warred across her features, but she didn't pull out of my grip. If anything, her fingers tightened around mine. "Thank you."

Genuine gratitude laced her words, and my breath stuttered at the sincerity coloring her features.

Without a response, I pulled, leading the girl and her protector out of the labyrinth.

"You promised you'd alert me before they destroyed the

hound," a man said, his voice wavering with menace. "This is absolutely unacceptable."

I had heard the voice once or twice before, but it was otherwise unfamiliar to me. Max's breath hitched, so I assumed she was better acquainted.

"I'm sorry, Cy. I didn't think they were going to actually do it tonight. My safehouse only just confirmed they'd take him." Another voice, this one I knew.

"He was here to protect her, and we were supposed to protect him."

Just a moment before they rounded the corner, I pulled Max into a small closet, the hound following close behind. She was pressed flush against my body, and I struggled to keep from pulling her closer. It took all of my focus to ignore the smell of the drying blood that coated her wrist and palm. We listened in silence as the protectors ran through the halls. I needed to hurry if I wanted to make it out of here alive. But even after I could no longer hear the two men, I couldn't seem to disentangle myself from the girl.

"That was Cyrus," she said, a layer of concern and confusion in her words. Her head shook against me, like she was tossing the frustration aside. "What—what's your name?"

I could feel, rather than see her chest pressing into my stomach as she looked up at me.

"We need to go now," I said. I pushed open the door and dragged her down the hall, not stopping until we reached an exit sign. When I turned back to look at her, she had a hand fisted in the hellhound's thick fur.

Another mystery. Hellhounds hated to be touched, and to be treated like a common house pet? What kind of magic did this girl weave?

I leaned into the heavy door, pleased when it opened to an unoccupied field, not far from a tick line of trees. Freedom was so close my mouth salivated. I gave myself one moment, just one, to savor the scent of the air, to feel the lush grass between my toes, to hold the hand of a pretty girl. It had been so long since I'd had any of these sensations, that my most vivid fantasies had not done them justice.

"Where will you go?" she asked.

I turned to her, her forehead creased with concern as she pulled her hand from mine. For a moment, I was tempted to tighten my grip, to pull her closer, to bring her with me. I wanted to unravel the mystery that had woven her in its web. But I didn't think I could do that without kidnapping her. And if I wanted to escape the protectors for good, bringing along one of them as my hostage—particularly one of their women—was not a great start.

Her words filtered through my mind as I let those thoughts float away. Where would I go? My contacts and friends would be difficult to trace down after all of this time. The world was different and I would need time to reorient myself. My world, and the people in it, changed quickly. Who knew what the state of things was now?

I shrugged, unable to offer her more explanation. I'd figure it out as I ran. And I'd run quite possibly forever.

She turned to her hellhound, and I watched in awe as the creature nudged her with its enormous head. Strange that the force didn't immediately knock her down. She was stronger than she looked. Good, she would need strength. The world had a lot in store for her, of that much I was sure.

"I'll make sure your hound gets out safely," I found myself saying. And again, I surprised myself by meaning it. While I agreed to lead her to the hound if she let me out of my cage, I suddenly wanted to see it through. It would be a piece of this place that I could take with me, maybe the only piece that wasn't filled with pain and absolute boredom. And the beast was important to her. I found myself wanting to give it a chance at survival if possible.

Her dark eyes narrowed, her face twisted with distrust. I didn't blame her. Our species did not interact, did not offer allyship. Of course to be honest, even if I were to go back on my word, she didn't have much to worry about. Vampires were strong, and I was as wily as the best of them, but we didn't stand a chance against a hellhound bent on our destruction.

"Just, you know, make sure the beast doesn't try to eat me," I added, offering a smirk even though I was only half in jest. Maybe she really could communicate with him, I'd seen stranger things.

She nodded once, resolve morphing her features into an expression of stunning fortitude. "I'll see you both to the edge of campus then."

We walked in silence for a long mile, just breathing in the clear night air. It was exhilarating and I almost regretted having to leave my unlikely new partner-in-crime behind. I found something about her quiet presence simultaneously soothing and motivating.

When we reached an unremarkable middle point in the forest, she stopped. She looked from me to the hound, her eyes lingering on the beast briefly before she collapsed all of her weight against it. I could hear soft weeping and tried to give them privacy. She mumbled empty platitudes like "be safe," and "thank you," and all sorts of nonsense. I had to physically keep from rolling my eyes, but the beast seemed to be soaking the attention up and I was unwilling to get on his bad side this close to freedom.

When she pulled back from the hound, her dark, watery eyes landed on me. "You too. Be safe," she said, and suddenly the words didn't feel so empty or meaningless. "And try not to, you know, eat people."

Figuring this would be my last chance to explore her odd draw, I stepped up to her, my heart picking up as she swallowed a gasp, and pressed my lips to hers. I'd had many women in my time, and maybe it was just the dry spell, or the invigoration of a prison escape, but something about the taste of her lips, the feel of her body pressed against mine, felt like being reborn, like my world was realigning in some fundamental way. Briefly, I thought she might give into the moment, but just as her lips started to respond to mine, she pushed away. She looked at me with confusion and betrayal but also with a lingering heat. Interesting.

I touched her face softly once more, smiling when she pulled away further. Her heart was racing, even more so than it had been while we were breaking out. She was more affected by the kiss than she was willing to let on.

And then, suddenly, I was aware of another heartbeat, not five hundred feet from us. "My name is Darius," I said, digging my feet into the dirt, ready to spring. "Until we meet again, little protector."

With one last lingering look, I took off in a run, pulling the crisp night air into my lungs, mildly aware of the four-legged beast following in pursuit.

16

ATLAS

I stopped dead, prepared to lunge. The vampire's hand was threaded through Max's hair, it's vile lips pressed against hers. Anger boiled through my blood and I breathed in and out, focusing on the air around me as it filtered through my lungs, trying to maintain control for as long as possible. What the hell was she doing, allowing that fucking creature to touch her?

When Seamus alerted us that the hellhound escaped, I knew that Max-fucking-Bentley would be the root cause of it. I knew that she had a soft spot for the hound, but a vampire? What the hell was she thinking?

And how was she standing there now, still alive? I stood as still as I could, for fear the creature would rip her throat out and drain her dry in front of me. Every muscle from my head down to my toes wanted to decapitate him. Right here, right now. Instead, I fought every urge, every instinct I had, and waited. It was only a moment—one second she was in his arms, and then she was pushing him away—but in that time, my stomach turned to stone and I bit a fresh wound into my tongue, the taste of copper and the warmth of blood filling my mouth.

The vamp's eyes locked on mine, an arched brow over

mismatched eyes like he was issuing a challenge. My limbs shook, begging to rip him apart, but I had to be smart about this. If I made the wrong move, Max would be collateral damage. And I wasn't exactly fighting at one-hundred percent tonight, my body exhausted and drained from our earlier mission. I wasn't sure if I could take him on solo.

Before I could decide what to do, the vampire and hellhound took off at a pace I could never match, not in my current state, not alone.

I took a step forward, tempted to at least try a pursuit, but the twig snapping underneath my foot startled Max. Her now-familiar dark eyes tore into me, a mixture of fear and confusion. Was she afraid of the vampire or afraid of me?

The thought that she could be in the arms of a vampire one moment and afraid of me the next stung like a bullet.

I stilled instantly, and raised my hands in surrender. I didn't have the composure to deal with this shit in a helpful way. Wade was awake and home and all I wanted to do was sink into a chair by his bed and linger in my relief. Just one fucking night of peace —was that too much to ask?

"Atlas," she said, the word coming out on a heavy breath. "It's not what you think. I swear."

"Really?" I couldn't keep the anger from my tone, but I balled my hands into fists to keep it as subtle as I could. "Because it looks like you broke out two dangerous creatures and made out with one of them."

She shook her head, her long hair sending a plume of her uniquely frustrating scent into the air. Her legs moved back slowly, one after the other.

She was scared, terrified even. And moving away from me and towards the vampire.

"They were going to kill Ralph. I had to get him out of there. And I needed Darius to help."

Darius. She called the fucking vampire by its name?

Her long, thin fingers unconsciously traced her bottom lip.

Part of me wanted to erase that memory from her mouth, remove his touch from her skin.

I tilted my head, my jaw clamped tight with tension. My lungs filled with a deep breath and I counted to five, clocking the chill of the air, the dark shadows of the forest, the smell of —her.

I took a step towards her and nodded in the direction of the cabin. I couldn't do this out here, not like this. I needed to get her safe, get her home. And then we'd start up a hunt. Until then, I was on babysitting duty. And I was not returning home unless she walked through that door with me. Not now, not tonight.

"Atlas, are you okay?" she asked, moving towards me suddenly in a rush. She reached one of her small hands towards my side, her face the fucking picture of concern. "Did you find the wolf tonight? Are you hurt?"

I lurched away from her touch, hissing through my teeth as pain coursed through my body. "We're going home," I said, turning to walk away, each step in sync with my racing heartbeat. "Now." I didn't bother turning around, I knew she would follow.

Neither of us spoke a single word during the walk back, but I could hear her heart pounding. I kept my ears peeled just in case the vampire or hound doubled back for her or initiated an attack, but on some level, I knew that they were long gone. Good, the chase would be better if I had to work for it.

I threw open the door, alerting everyone to our presence, to my anger. Declan and Eli came hammering down the staircase within moments, Eli's hair mussed up from his pillow. Declan looked as alert and moody as ever with that don't-fuck-with-me expression she always wore, even to bed.

"Max?" Eli said, his voice still raspy with sleep. "How'd you get down here so fast?"

"She was already down here," Declan said, running a frustrated hand through her long hair, pulling in frustration when her fingers latched onto a tangle. "She fucking snuck out like a damn twelve-year-old."

I could feel Max shuffling to the side, cowering a bit in my shadow, like I'd protect her from Dec's wrath.

"No way," Eli said, and then he turned back up the stairs, disappearing from sight. "I literally checked up on her half an hour ago." His voice was muffled as he combed through the house, likely storming into Sarah's old room. "Pillows? Seriously? I can't believe I fell for that. Wait until my dad hears." He came jogging back to the stairs, a disbelieving grin on his face. "He'll be so pleased someone's pulled that trick over on me—after all the times I've had him pulling his hair out from the same thing."

"How'd you find her?" Declan asked, taking a few steps towards us. She was glaring daggers at Max. I'd been on the bad end of that glare enough times to understand why Max was sinking back towards the door.

Max took a large breath in, like she was talking herself into something, and then she stepped out from behind my back and into the entryway. "Look, I'm sorry that I snuck out. You're right. That wasn't cool."

Eli started to nod, opening his mouth to agree, but slammed it shut when she continued.

"But none of you are my parents, nor are you my keepers. You all made it more than clear you didn't want to deal with me tagging along." She shook her head, flinging her hair out of her face. "And that's totally fine. Really, I mean it. I get it. I came into your home and was inserted into the team, however temporarily. And you didn't ask for that. So I'm sorry that I didn't tell you I was leaving before I left. But I'm not sorry that I left, and I'm not going to pretend that I am."

I bit back a grin as she crossed her arms defiantly, at the way that Declan's nostrils flared at her stubbornness. About time someone gave her a run for her money. In fact, I was halfway to forgiving her myself until I remembered the vampire and the whole reason she snuck out in the first place.

"So," Eli said, "where were you then? Some party in a dorm we didn't know about? Or did you go back to Jer?"

Jer. Just the name of that entitled asshole had my hackles rising. When you knew someone their entire life, it was easy to know all the parts of them—even the truly vile ones.

"I broke into the lab to let Ralph out," Max said, her chin jutting up, a challenge in her eyes. She was holding her own, no longer sinking back, I'd give her that much.

Eli arched a brow, clearly impressed. And he had reason to be, we all did, considering all the times we'd snuck down there over the years to spy on the creatures we'd be tasked with capturing. "Who's Ralph?"

"My hellhound," she said, rolling her teeth gently over her bottom lip. She seemed to do that a lot when she was nervous.

I hated the fact that I noticed, that my eyes snagged on the gesture every single time.

"She succeeded," I said, watching their eyes widen in shock. "And," I added, "she intentionally let one of the vampires out too."

"She fucking did what?" The fury on Declan's face sharpened her already otherworldly features. She looked like an angel of death. I hadn't seen her this angry in a long while. Not since we were kids.

Max unconsciously took a step back in my direction. She didn't understand her reaction, which was part of the problem. Naive girl was new to this world and she went around trusting everyone and everything she encountered. She had no idea what surviving in our world required. Honestly, she was lucky she'd made it as long as she had.

"Seriously?" Eli said, his neck reddening with anger. I was surprised to see him so pissed. He was definitely the most laid back of all of us, and usually found it exciting when someone survived a close call. "You could've been killed, Max. I get wanting to save the hellhound or whatever. But a fucking vampire? Do you have any idea how lucky you are? How could you be so reckless?" He paced up and down the entryway, shaking his head as he spoke, his body practically vibrating with anxious energy.

I almost revealed that she'd let the creature kiss her, but the thought still made me angry enough that I didn't want to revisit the visual any time soon. That'd be a discussion for another day.

"You almost died from a vamp attack," Dec said, reigning in her anger until her words sounded clipped and flat. "You get that, right? A few weeks ago, you almost died." She nodded her head towards the staircase as she studied Max with a precise, cold fury. "And Wade, he also just almost died from a vamp attack. So while you're standing there all haughty and proud of yourself for unleashing some unknown dog into the wild, know that whoever that vamp kills while he's on the run—that's on you. That blood is on your hands." She turned, ran up the stairs, and slammed her door.

A loud crash upstairs made Max jump. She'd shrunken down a bit, and for the first time looked like she felt guilty for more than letting the vampire touch her. Good. Protectors were supposed to protect each other and other humans, not endanger them. Maybe Declan's reality check would affect her actions in a way nothing else would.

Eli and Max stood in a silent standoff until she backed down and went into her room, a much softer door slam echoing throughout the cabin. Poor Wade, if he'd been asleep before, there was no way he was now.

Still collecting myself, and trying to cool down enough to have a conversation, I hammered a text to Seamus, alerting him of the evening's turn of events.

Eli turned into the kitchen and I heard the welcome hiss as he popped the lid off two beers. Hopefully it would help take the edge off. I was mad as hell, but there was so much else warring in me right now that I didn't have the time or energy to deal with it all. That was for another day. Beer would be good, beer I could focus on.

My phone vibrated and I followed Eli into the kitchen, reading. "Seamus wants us to keep her on lockdown here. He's going to grab Cyrus but doesn't want to alert anyone else. He's afraid they'll be kicked out or that Max will face radical discipline for her actions."

Eli's brows knit together as he downed half his beer in a single gulp. "What does that mean? Radical discipline? What would they do to her?"

I let out a long breath, mimicking his action. "It means that it's on Seamus, Cyrus, and us to get this vamp and hellhound back in the lab. Before too many people realize there was a breach in the first place."

"Before Alleva finds out, you mean," Eli said, his knuckles were white and I half-expected him to shatter the bottle.

I nodded, exhaustion seeping through my bones. I wanted nothing more than to sleep for the next three days. But instead, we were going on a hunt.

17

MAX

I tried for hours to sleep, but the harder I seemed to chase it, the more rest seemed to evade me. Sleep was annoying that way. All I could think about was whether or not Ralph was okay. It was a lot easier to focus on his safety than on the fact that I'd kissed a freaking vampire. And that the two seconds of lip-to-lip action was eons better than what I'd had with Michael. What the hell was wrong with me?

In the span of twenty-four hours I'd essentially made out with two different people—both of whom ran off immediately after. Granted, I didn't want Darius to stick around. My brain was muddled and confused enough as it was already.

With a final huff, I pushed myself up in bed. My eyes had adjusted to the dark and I studied Sarah's old room for a moment: the outlines of books on her shelves, her record player and interesting collection of music, the large window that overlooked the trees. I allowed myself to wonder just briefly what living with them was like for her. Did they welcome her? Did they want her to be part of their team? Or was she on the outside of their club, like me? Still, no matter how pissed I got with Atlas or Declan or Eli, I couldn't deny that some part of me was infuriatingly drawn to them all. Drawn to them in a way that

FORGING THE GUILD

I hadn't been drawn to Ten, no matter how much better I got along with Arnell and his team.

Something about Atlas and the rest of them had carved its way underneath my skin, and no matter how much I wanted to, I couldn't seem to shake it. Even though I didn't regret breaking Ralph out, the look on Declan's face, her absolute disappointment with me, was permanently tattooed on the back of my eyelids. I didn't know if she'd be capable of forgiving me, but as soon as a crippling fear that she wouldn't consumed my thoughts, I realized how desperately I wanted her to.

Hopefully everyone in the house was passed out by now, so I could sneak down for some water and a late night snack without having to stomach any more incriminating glares and speeches. Jailbreaks made me famished.

When I tried to turn the doorknob, it didn't budge. They'd locked me in, then. Can't say that I completely blamed them if I was being honest with myself. I was pretty sure that freeing a vampire was a serious crime and I knew I'd have to deal with the repercussions eventually. For now, that apparently meant house arrest.

And while I didn't want to think about Darius, Declan had a point. Anyone he harmed—that was on me. I was definitely not prepared to handle that level of guilt. For now, I'd push it down and out of my mind, hoping like hell that wherever he was, he wasn't hurting anyone. As much as I hated vampires, Darius just hadn't seemed that, I don't know, evil? If I lingered for too long on our conversations, it felt like he was just another person trapped up in this world of angels and demons. Maybe I just expected vampires to be more like mindless zombies, or clearly hellbent on attacking me like the guy at Vanish or the girl in the lab.

It was a ridiculous sentiment though, considering I literally watched Darius snap a protector's neck. Granted, that protector was two seconds away from killing Ralph, but still.

He ate him. And that death blow might as well have been cast by my own hand.

The weight of that realization gripped my lungs and I forced myself to breathe in and out in deep, long breaths. My eyes blurred with dancing dots of light as a dull beeping sound rang through my ears. It took all of my attention to keep from throwing up all over Sarah's pretty carpet—to focus on anything but the fact that a protector was dead tonight because of me.

Ro. I needed to get to Ro. He would know how to make this better, make things okay. He could tell me what to do or next or at least keep me company until Cyrus and Seamus came to deliver whatever punishment they saw fit—whatever it was, I knew in the very marrow of my bones that I deserved it.

It was weird. My whole life I'd thought about becoming a protector one day, about keeping humans safe from the monsters that went bump in the night. Only it turned out that I was the one who let those monsters free to terrorize them. In one night, I watched my future and my career tumble like Jenga blocks. There was no belonging for me now, not really.

But at least Ralph was safe. He'd make it back to wherever his home was. At least his death wasn't on my hands—it wasn't enough to quell my shame, but it was something.

I grabbed my bag and shuffled around until I found the small pouch I was looking for. Cyrus taught us the importance of fighting, sure, but he'd also made sure that we knew how to pick a lock. He'd made it clear that sometimes knowing how and when to escape danger was just as important as fighting through it.

I rifled through my kit until I found the tools I was looking for and made quick work of the lock mechanism. It was easier than most, and probably could have been managed without my kit, just the proper use of leverage. Bedroom doors didn't usually come with top-level security needs.

The latch popped softly, and I crept out, not wanting to disturb the team or rehash our argument. If they wanted to yell at me some more tomorrow, that was fine—Ralph would be long gone and that was all that mattered right now. I would take my punishment standing tall.

The hall was dark and I still didn't have the layout of everything in the cabin memorized, so I pressed my hand against the wall as a guide. It was working well until I stubbed my toe on a door frame—if I remembered correctly, it was Wade's—and bit back a whimper.

I held my breath and stopped moving, hoping the small noise didn't wake anyone.

I heard shuffling on the other side of the door, but when it stopped, I started moving again.

Until, all at once, the door swung open and I was pressed against the wall. One moment, I was alone and bumbling around, the next Wade's body was leaning into me, a knife pressed against the soft skin of my neck.

"Max?" He exhaled, relinquishing the grip on his knife. He took a step back to give me some space and I instantly felt the chill of his absence. "What the hell are you doing up?" He rubbed sleep from his eyes and shook his head. "You were supposed to be locked in for the night. Jesus, I thought you were —I could have killed you, you know?"

He wasn't whispering and I was surprised no one else came out to check on the commotion. Wade had woken up instantly.

"I grew up with Cyrus," I said, not needing to offer any more of an explanation.

He leaned against the wall, and even in the dark I could see soft perspiration across the smooth skin of his forehead. He was winded, just from standing up and rushing to the hallway.

Rest. After his ordeal, he desperately needed rest.

"Come on." I grabbed his arm and threw it across my shoulders, letting his weight fall on me. "You shouldn't be up, you're going to use what little energy you have chasing me around in the dark. Let's get you back to bed."

He let me lead him into his room, and I helped him get readjusted in bed, covering his lap with his blankets and fluffing his pillows.

He turned on a small bedside lamp, the soft light distorting his features slightly and making him look even more drained than I'd realized.

Unable to stop myself, I rested my palm against his cheek, suddenly needing to feel his skin, needing to know that he was okay.

"I hate being this weak," he said, his frustration leaking into his voice, but he didn't pull away from me.

"You just woke up today, Wade." I sat next to him on his bed and grabbed the glass of water on his nightstand. "Drink this, you need to take it easy. You'll be back to normal in no time, but until then, you need to be kind to yourself. Relax. Let everyone take care of you for once, okay?"

His pale blue eyes studied me as he grabbed the glass and I caught my breath as his fingers brushed against mine. "I'm glad you're okay, Max."

I exhaled sharply, instantly breaking eye contact. It was too much. This whole night, hell this whole week, was too much. "That makes one of you, the rest of your team seems to hate me for what I did."

Wade shrugged, a hardness to his features that I wasn't used to. "Do you blame them? I get that you wanted to protect the hellhound. Really, I do." He set the glass back down, missing the coaster, and grabbed my hand. "But you let out a dangerous vampire. A killer. One protector is dead, and who knows how many more he'll kill before they get him back." His jaw clenched as he shook his head softly. "Jesus, Max. I mean do you realize how lucky you are that you're still alive? What were you thinking?"

That familiar, awful feeling churned in my gut again and I studied the worn books on his shelf, unable to meet his eyes with mine. We sat in silence for a few minutes, but I could feel Wade's gaze as he studied me. I knew he wanted me to say something, to make it better, but I couldn't. I didn't know where to start.

Breaking the tension, I nodded towards the door.

"Everyone else a heavy sleeper around here or what?" I asked, my attempt at humor falling flat.

An unreadable expression crossed his face, disappointment maybe or frustration? "They're out."

My breath caught the second that I realized what that meant. "They're going after them?"

Wade didn't answer, but his silence was enough. I saw it in the flare of his nose, the clench of his jaw—he was angry with himself, for being stuck here watching me. He wanted to be out with his team, helping them hunt the monsters down.

Were they going after Ralph or just Darius? Were they still together? My heartrate started picking up and I stood quickly, dizzy with fear. There was no way that I went through what I went through tonight—no way that I threw everything I stood for away, just for Ralph to end up back here as a decomposing body.

I understood why they needed to go after Darius, I did. It was our job, what we were designed and trained to do. But Ralph was not a murderer. He didn't belong in a cage. He didn't deserve to be executed.

Wade watched the decision settle on my features just a second too late. Before he reached his arm out to stop me, I was halfway through the door.

"Max," he said, using his remaining energy to stand next to his bed. "Please just let them handle it. Stay here, please. I can't watch out for you if you leave."

"Sorry, Wade," I said, and I was. I wanted to stay with him, to be part of their team and fit in with the protectors here. But this was too important. And I realized now that I didn't fit here, and maybe never would.

Without another look, I tore down the stairs, stopping just long enough to shove my feet into my sneakers.

"Max, wait. Please," Wade said, his voice echoing down the hall. I felt bad leaving him, especially considering he wasn't in great shape and no one was around. But this was life or death and there was no way I was letting Ralph get roped back into his doom, even if it meant I had to use Wade's current condition to my advantage. I'd find a way to make it up to him eventually.

I hoped I would anyway. There wasn't another option.

When I reached the trail of trees, the breeze blowing my hair in every direction, I discovered another problem. I didn't exactly know where the guys were. I knew where the line to the property was and vaguely which direction Darius took off in, but I wasn't exactly familiar with these surroundings. And I didn't have a great sense of direction.

I let out a frustrated grunt as I looked from one tree to another, angry with myself for what felt like the millionth time tonight. Without second guessing myself, I ran to Ten's cabin, pounding on the door until a disgruntled Sharla answered, her hair wrapped tightly in silk.

"I need my brother, now," I said, my words coming out with an edge of desperation. I felt bad skipping pleasantries, but Sharla's expression sharpened as she sensed my emergency. As soon as she processed my request, she went tearing back into the house.

I counted the seconds until Ro was standing in front of me—exactly thirty-seven—with a focused and alert expression on his face, like I hadn't just woken him up in the middle of the night. With a single nod, I turned and ran, thankful when I heard his familiar, heavy steps following behind me. Trusting my gut, I ran with all of my stamina, all of my strength to the spot I last saw Ralph and Darius. My feet dug into the soft ground, kicking up small puffs of dirt as I pumped my arms and explained the situation to Ro through chaotic bursts of breath.

He didn't voice his frustration, but I could feel his glare nailing the back of my head, no doubt pissed that I went through with the rescue mission on my own. Still, he listened to every word, every twist of the story without directly calling me out. He knew I was aware that I messed up tonight, on several counts.

"I'm sorry," I breathed out. I winced at the terror in my tone and pushed my body faster. "It was poorly planned, and I'm sorry I didn't bring you in the first place. I don't know what I was thinking. But Ro, please. I need you to not be mad and just help me track them down. You can kick my ass tomorrow and the day after that. But not tonight."

I looked out of the corner of my eye, my heart melting with relief when he gave me a single nod, determination dissolving the leftover hurt and anger on his face.

The night air was cool and I willed myself to focus on the familiar pattern of trees. I knew which direction Darius and Ralph had gone, so I would just take the same path and hope we found them. Eventually.

The winding paths through the woods all started to blur together, so I relied on Ro to track. It was infuriating watching him work, bending over snapped twigs, using his phone to shine a light on random indentations in the dirt—all while I stood, useless and filled with an anxiety so deep it was palpable.

We moved for what felt like hours, but I knew it was likely just minutes. Time didn't make sense, didn't follow rules in moments like these.

Ro stopped, and I studied as he tilted his head, face scrunched in confusion.

"What?" I asked, breathless, studying the twigs and bark around me like I could Sherlock whatever conclusion he'd drawn until it landed me in front of a safe and happy Ralph.

"The trail doesn't make sense here," he said, bending down and pointing to a random sweep of leaves and footprints.

It meant nothing to me and frustration with my own inadequacies made me snap. "Ro, we don't have time for this to become a school lesson, just spit it out."

He shot me a look and I withered in shame, my stomach

clenching in an unforgiving knot.

"I'm sorry," I said, "it's just, if Ralph dies, it's on me. And I can't handle another death on my hands tonight. I don't know how I'd survive it."

Ro nodded once and stood back up from his crouch. "They were here, I see four sets of footprints, and one set of pawprints." He paused, doubt creating a crease between his brows. "But then it becomes another set of pawprints, and the third person's footprints disappear. There's no dragging though, so it's like they were attacked by another beast but then just disappeared completely or were lifted into the air."

"That doesn't make any sense," I said, digging half crescents into the soft flesh of my palms.

"I know," Ro said, his face smoothing out in concentration. He started walking further into the woods, muscles tense with focus, not uttering another word or theory out loud.

We continued on for I don't know how long—time started to disappear and grow hazy with tension.

I was close to giving up altogether when a large shadow cut off our path. My breath hitched and I let out a thankful, desperate laugh. I ran towards the large, shaggy dog, and threw my arms around his neck. He should have been long gone by now—running back home. Instead, he was here. I just had to be happy that we found him before anyone else did.

"You're okay," I said, breathing in the now-familiar, woody scent of the hellhound.

Ralph's large tongue swept up the side of my face, but I was so relieved to see him that I didn't even care about the slobber. He let out a playful chirp when he saw Ro, but then moved away from us, dragging us deeper into the forest.

Ro's fist clamped around my sleeve, stopping me from following him just yet.

"Max, we found him. We should hide him and then get the hell out of here," Ro said, his eyes moving side-to-side as he studied every shadow, every tree. "Something doesn't feel right."

The woods around us were silent, except for the calming sound of the wind sweeping through some leaves, so I ignored Ro, and went tearing after Ralph—he'd picked up speed during Ro's hesitation, and while I was fast, I wasn't hellhound-fast.

We came into a small clearing, grass trampled from a fight, to find Declan and Eli pinning Darius down to the ground. It looked like they'd injected him with something, because his eyes were hazy and he shot me a loopy smile as we trudged closer. Part of me wanted to peel them off of him and check to make sure he was okay, that they hadn't done any permanent damage. But I stamped that impulse down as quickly as I could, flashes of the dead protector floating through my mind. Atlas, Declan, all of the guys—they were right. Darius was a killer and the brief allyship he'd shown me was just that, brief. He needed me and I needed him but that alliance was over. And I was kidding myself if I thought he wouldn't go ripping through humans the second they let him up.

"Max?" Declan's voice held an air of surprise, but was gruff with exertion—even though it was a losing battle, Darius fought against the effects of the injection. "Damnit Max, get the hell out of here. Do you not follow any instructions? You're going to get yourself and everyone else killed."

The leaves to the left of them rustled and I reached to my thigh to grab a throwing knife.

I came up empty. In my rush to get out of the house before Wade could stop me, I'd forgotten to grab a weapon. Careless mistake. Such a careless fucking mistake.

A breath of air pushed through my teeth in relief when the branches moved to the side revealing Atlas. "Atlas," I said, letting out an alarmed chuckle. "You scared the shit out of me."

He was wearing nothing but a loose pair of shorts and his eyes were almost completely yellow, levelling me with a glare that knocked the wind out of me more than Reza's fist had. Next to me, Ralph tensed, his lips pulled back to reveal a set of sharp, terrifying teeth. It was the first time since I'd encountered him that he looked the part of hellhound, filled with fury and menace. I took a step back, alarmed by the transformation and watched as he crept between me and the guys, like he was trying to protect me from them.

I stuck out a hesitant hand and rested it on Ralph's back. "Easy, boy. They won't hurt us, it's okay." I hoped like hell that they'd let Ralph go, now that they had Darius under control. Their focus definitely seemed targeted on Darius, but a rush of frustration beat behind my eyes at the realization that Ralph drew himself straight to them. It was like he was trying to get thrown back in the lab cellar.

"What the hell's wrong with him?" Ro asked. I felt the breath of his words against the back of my neck and could hear the layer of fear in his quiet, usually calm voice.

I shook my head and studied the members of Six. Declan and Eli looked from Atlas to me and Ro, unreadable expressions on their faces. I took a step forward, standing beside Ralph and studied Atlas. Something about that gold tinge in his eyes unsettled me; they were so bright now that they were almost glowing. His chest was pumping hard with heavy breaths as he pressed his hand into a wound on his side. His abdomen was wet with blood.

I dug my hand hard into Ralph's thick fur, my breath coming out in quick gasps, like my body was filling things in just a second before my mind. My mind raced, cataloguing all of the pieces: the first night I met Ralph, the mystery scar on Atlas's arm, Jer's blade tonight, the secrecy and mood swings, the way Eli and Declan acted around the wolf earlier tonight.

Those eyes.

Those fucking eyes.

My feet started moving back, one step and then two as I shook my head. "Oh my god," I breathed out, a small sob breaking through. "It's you. This whole time, it's been you."

I shook my head, turned, grabbed Ro's hand, and took off into a run as Ralph trailed behind us.

Atlas was a fucking werewolf.

18
MAX

My forehead was slick with sweat as I ran, my feet pounding into the soft ground. I wasn't entirely sure where I was leading Ro and Ralph, whether we were going back towards The Guild or farther away, but I needed to be anywhere but where we were.

All of this time it was Atlas. I had been living with a werewolf. And they had the audacity to be mad at me for letting a vampire out of a cage? Did Seamus know? Did Alleva? Was I the only one left in the dark on what Atlas really was?

It felt like I was living in a bad episode of Teen Wolf. Ro's steady breathing as he followed helped lull me back to reality, back to something familiar and understandable and normal.

"Max, what the hell are we doing?" Ro asked, his arms pumping at his sides as he tried to keep up with my frantic pace as I zigzagged here and then there. "Where are we going?"

I shook my head, unable to offer any more explanation, grateful when the gesture stopped further questions.

A loud laugh echoed through the trees, and I skidded to a halt, only half aware of Ro's body colliding with mine as we went crashing down.

"You okay?" he asked, giving me a hand up from the ground where I'd landed. "What was that?"

I watched him as the confusion in his eyes transformed into determined focus. He was scanning the area around us as he pulled me to my feet. Dusting stray dirt and leaves from my butt, I followed suit. That laugh didn't belong to Declan or either of the guys and I looked a few feet over to Ralph. He seemed two steps ahead of the situation at all times, and what I saw when I looked at him sunk dread into my belly.

His hackles were up, a low, menacing growl emanating from his chest.

I looked from the direction he was pointed towards the trees and stifled a scream. Four figures were walking towards us— three men and a woman. There was something in the way they carried themselves that was just a bit off. The girl's limbs were contorting and bending in odd directions. Gray fur lined her arms and I watched in morbid fascination as her fingers curved into claws. I'd never seen a wolf transform before.

I swallowed my gasp as Ro and I instinctively moved towards each other, for comfort and protection. I scanned the surroundings for something that could be construed as a weapon. I wasn't sure if the other three were vampires, wolves, or what. Either way, our options for defending ourselves were pretty limited.

Shit, shit, shit. This night was like a never-ending dream from hell.

Ro's large hand swallowed mine, and I ignored the knot in my throat when he squeezed. His body was steady, but I could feel the small tremor in his hand. He was scared. And I was the reason he was here. We were going to die and it was all my fault.

The realization that I would be the cause of my brother's death stole my breath and I blinked away the glossy lining of tears in my eyes.

Pulling my hand from his, I looked into his face, trying to memorize every angle and expression. He was the most important person in the world to me, and it would be worth my life if I could save his.

"You need to go," I said, my words coming out in a soft croak.

He shook his head, anger creating familiar lines through his forehead. "Don't be ridiculous."

"Listen, Ro." I nodded towards Ralph. "I have protection. You need to run, you need to go get help. Ralph and I can stay here, distract them until you get back, and you can go find somebody. Anybody. Even Atlas." I didn't trust Atlas, but he hadn't killed me yet, no matter how often he looked like he wanted to, so maybe he wasn't completely evil. It was a risk I was willing to take right now. "We have to stop them before they get into town or to The Guild. We need backup. And now, or else too many people will die tonight."

"Fine," he said, resolve steeling his voice. He knew I was right—that if we both died here, these creatures would go attack and kill more people. "You go then and I'll distract them."

I let out a puff of air, not surprised by his stubbornness but annoyed all the same. We didn't have time for this.

I would be stubborn too, leave him no option but to leave us here and go get help. We both knew that he had a better chance of retracing our steps anyway. My tracking skills were shit.

I looked at Ralph, and it was like he could see my plan as it unfolded in my mind. With a nod, we went bounding through the trees, towards the group of creatures. I grabbed a large branch on the way, but I wasn't dense enough to think it would do much more than cause a temporary distraction or annoyance. A twig up against a werewolf would be nothing more than a pathetic game of fetch, with my bones as a nice tasty reward.

"Jesus, Max," Ro whisper-yelled behind us. "Just. Don't die." I heard the fear lodge in his throat as I choked back tears. "I'll be right back in two minutes. Seriously, I'll kill you if you're not still alive. Bring you back and kill you." He was already tearing off in the direction we'd come from, faster than I'd ever seen him run before.

A small smile crossed my face when the four creatures focused on me. Ro stood a chance, if I could keep them occupied for a few minutes, he'd be okay. That was enough.

More than enough. It was all I needed.

My body collided with the female wolf just as she shook her head, the final pieces of her humanity slipping away. She was smaller than Atlas's wolf had been. Small mercies.

We collapsed in a pile of bones and limbs and I felt, rather than saw, Ralph going after the others. His long, deep howl resonated through the air in a bone-shaking battle cry.

My fists rammed into the wolf's ribs as I kept her underneath me. It took all of my strength to keep her teeth twisted away from my thigh, but I kicked my left leg and felt her jaw snap.

I bit back a grin at the satisfying crunch of bone. I couldn't do much without a dagger, but I'd do what I could for as long as I could.

Her high whine alerted her companions and I paused just long enough to look up. Ralph was head-to-head with another wolf, this one brown and slightly larger than the girl, maybe by thirty or forty pounds. The other two still looked like men and I had a feeling they were vampires. I briefly wondered whether this was the group Wade had encountered, but shook the thought away quickly. It didn't matter right now.

One of the men turned towards me and the she-wolf, eyes narrowing in anger while the other advanced on Ralph and the other wolf.

The clash had gone on less than a few seconds, but it was like I was watching it all unfold in slow-motion, a macabre protraction of my eventual death.

Using her as a jumping board, I leapt off the wolf, backing up a few steps. Her claws had decimated the material of my leggings, and I was vaguely aware of blood dripping from my arm. I fisted my fingers, pleased that no bones felt broken.

Maybe I could hold this vampire and wolf back long enough for Ro to return with help.

Maybe.

"Looks like your friend abandoned you, girl," the vampire said, his dark eyes watching the blood drip down my arm with a sick hunger. "I always said protectors were an unreliable lot. Lucky for me, you'll make a nice appetizer."

His hair was dark, long, and pulled back into a low ponytail, and I was struck by how completely stereotypical he looked—it was like he'd walked off the set of a cheezy B movie.

I took several steps back, drawing him away from Ralph and the other two—I wanted Ralph to have as good of a chance as possible, so I'd keep these two occupied as best as I could.

The wolf pulled herself up next to the vamp, the two of them stalking towards me. Her gold eyes were focused, her lips pulled back. I could practically feel her rage soaking into every nerve of my body.

After a few minutes, they grew tired of their slow descent and simultaneously pounced. I stepped back and twisted, successfully pulling away from the wolf, but landing right underneath the vamp. His sharp teeth sank into my arm as I flailed underneath him and kneed him in the balls. His breath heated my neck as he grunted in pain, but it wasn't enough to get him to unlatch. The wolf no longer had a functional jaw, but she dug her claws into my shoulder and already-damaged arm. I could feel each nail as it sunk and pulled so deep that I knew she was gouging out chunks of bone.

Anger and adrenaline soared through my blood and I used every last ounce of energy I had to push the vampire off before he could sink his teeth in again. He was only a foot away from me, but I used the brief reprieve to throw my weight on top of the wolf and ram my only functional arm over and over against her already ruined muzzle. I vowed that I would kill one of them before they took me down. This time, I'd earn my fame for fighting off a hellbeast solo.

I looked back, surprised the vampire hadn't regained his footing and pulled me from his furry partner. A mixture of relief and fear rushed over me at what I saw, adrenaline running so high that I couldn't properly sort out my feelings.

"Wade." My voice croaked and caught on his name, raw with wear, and I realized belatedly that I must've been screaming during the attack.

His normally glowing complexion was pale and clammy, with droplets of sweat soaking through his t-shirt. He was exhausted just from standing earlier, so I had no idea how he'd managed to store up the energy to get out here. He must have followed me when I ran out on him. The thought alone punched harder into my gut and with more sting than the werewolf had managed.

Exhausted or not, he met the vampire blow-for-blow in a steady dance, his fingers clasped around a silver-coated blade as he tried to ward him off and push him away from reaching me. There was so much power emanating from him, even though I could see the energy draining from his limbs. He needed to go, he couldn't be here.

The realization that I'd endangered him so soon after his last brush with death twisted my stomach with a ragged, stormy guilt. I wouldn't leave Wade to fight the vampire alone, I couldn't give up, couldn't die on him. Not now.

We'd fight together and then we'd go home and I'd follow whatever rules Cyrus and Seamus saw fit. I was done resisting, done trying to prove myself. All I managed to do was fuck everything up.

Determination filled me and I felt along the ground for something, the branch I'd grabbed long abandoned. A grotesque grin spread across my lips as my fingers grazed the smooth surface of a large rock. I crawled over the wolf as she dug her claws into my side, completely oblivious to the pain, until I closed my good hand around it, fingers gripping with every ounce of my remaining strength.

With one huge breath, I lifted the stone above my head,

screaming in anguish as the pain made itself known in my left arm. Then, with one final surge of energy, I brought the rock down onto the wolf's skull with two heavy blows.

She stilled instantly. I wasn't sure if she could survive that, since I hadn't decapitated her, but she was unconscious, at least, which was good enough for now.

I rolled off her and looked at Ralph. The wolf lay in two pieces besides him, the head no longer attached to the body. Blood painted the ground, but none of it appeared to be the hellhound's. His large canines sank into the vamp's neck and I sighed in relief. Maybe we would all actually survive this.

As soon as the thought passed through my head, I saw the outlines of more creatures leaving the shadow of trees surrounding us. With a dull realization, my heart sank. There had to be at least ten more ready to join in on the fight. And all that I was armed with was a damn stone.

"No," I said, my voice dripping with defeat. We were doomed. I'd doomed us all. Why didn't I listen to Ro and just go back to the cabin with Ralph. I could've found a way to protect him and left it at that.

Wade turned around, his eyes searching for me and I saw the realization cross his features as soon as he saw the bodies surrounding us, closing us in their circle step by excruciating step.

They took their time, knowing we couldn't go anywhere. My body vibrated with fear and all I wanted to do was clasp my arms around Wade's neck and will us out of here—will us home.

Why was he here? Why did he have to come after me? Why didn't I just get a sip of water like I'd originally planned and then fall back asleep?

The vamp snuck up behind Wade as he stared in horror at our circle of doom and gripped his head. I ran with every ounce of energy I had left, desperate to reach him before the inevitable.

I was too far away to do anything, way too far. Tears clouded my vision until I could barely see Wade standing in front of me.

"Nooooo," I screamed as terror like I'd never known saturated every ounce of my being, seeping out of every single pore.

Wade's eyes found mine, their blue depths filled with a chilling acceptance and fear that would haunt me for as long as I breathed.

And then all I heard was the resounding *crack* as the vampire snapped his neck, like it was little more than a twig. It was quiet, but the sound ricocheted in my head as if it was my own spine breaking.

I watched, stunned, as Wade's body fell to the ground.

The noise of the battle slipped away—the sounds, the smells, all of it gone. Until all I could focus on was Wade's eyes, open and empty as they stared unseeing in my direction. This wasn't like before, he wasn't in a peaceful sleep, he wouldn't be brought to Greta for treatment. There wasn't any waking up from this.

An unrecognizable sob wrenched from my chest and lodged in my throat, until I was choking on the grief as it washed over me.

Wade was dead because of me.

He left the house, barely able to stand, and now he was on the ground in a lifeless heap.

My death didn't matter anymore, there was no surviving this agony, no surviving this abject misery.

No point.

19

ELI

I could feel my blood coursing through my veins as we moved across the forest, weaving through the trees. We followed Rowan's lead as we made our way towards Max, but no matter how fast we pushed, it didn't feel fast enough. His words were rushed and laced with terror as he'd explained what happened. I just hoped we weren't too late.

Please be alive. Just hold out for a little bit longer, we're almost there. Please, please, please.

My thoughts were racing like a whirlwind through my head. We should've gone after her as soon as she ran, as soon as she pieced together what Atlas was—though I didn't know how she did.

Something broke between us tonight, I knew it in my gut, could feel it as acutely as a knife; that look on her face when she figured it out almost cut me in half.

Complete dejection, fear, broken trust.

If only lying about Atlas was the only way I'd broken her trust this week. My stomach churned at the thought.

When she ran, Atlas said to give her some space. He saw the realization on her face as clear as day. We thought that the creepy lab vamp was the only thing out here that was any real threat to her. And we'd already taken him down.

Atlas was in his wolf form, so he reached the clearing just before the rest of us did, Rowan falling in line with me and Dec. If he was surprised or terrified by Atlas's transformation, he didn't show it—didn't even break his fucking stride. I searched through the bodies to find her. Rowan said there were only four, but as soon as we pushed past the trees, I counted at least a dozen. My eyes were drawn to Max like a moth to a flame, my breath stuttering in relief when I saw she was still alive, if barely.

"Max," Rowan screamed, as he pushed himself harder and faster to get to her. There was so much desperation in his voice —the sound achingly chilling.

Her clothes were torn and there was blood—so much blood —covering her head-to-toe. Just as soon as I found her, I saw Wade, positioned a few feet away from her as she ran screaming towards him. Atlas let out a heart wrenching sound, somewhere between a howl and a sob, as we saw it happen in slow motion, too far away for us to stop the dominoes. In a flash, the vampire snapped Wade's neck like he was nothing to him, little more than a toothpick.

Atlas's horrifying howl of grief shook me to my core as I dropped to my knees, my fingers digging into the dirt to keep me grounded.

Did that just happen? Was this real life? Maybe it was a trick of the light. I held onto that hope as I stood and surged forward, pushing my way towards them both.

Wade would be okay, it was a mistake, a weird angle, nothing more. We would get there, we'd fight them all off, he would be alive, then we'd go home and laugh about this later. Just like we always did after a close mission.

My heart beat a panicked song against my ribs as I pushed and pushed, fighting to get to them. I was vaguely aware of Declan and Rowan at my side, keeping pace, but I felt them more than saw them there.

Atlas was tearing through the clearing ahead of me, but long before he reached Wade, a tall man appeared, as if out of nowhere. He looked down at Wade's crumpled body with a small frown, picking him up like a bride. With a slow, meandering glance around at all of the creatures lying in wait, he studied the scene.

And then, as if hypnotized, the creatures in the clearing sank back into the forest, disappearing from sight.

The man looked down at Max with an unreadable expression in his dark eyes before disappearing.

He was there one second, and the next Atlas was soaring through where he'd just been standing, the clearing now empty except for the bloodied, battered hellhound and an even bloodier Max.

She stood, her eyes wide and filled with tears. Her legs wobbled uncontrollably, and I realized as I reached her just how torn up her body was.

"Wade," she said, the word nothing more than a whimper, hollow and chilling.

And then she collapsed.

I caught her at the last second, delirious with gratitude when I felt a soft pulse. She was alive. We'd sort through everything eventually, but she was alive. And for now that would have to be enough.

I cradled her against my chest as the hellhound limped over to us. He wasn't in the best shape, but he'd survive. His large muzzle inched towards Max and he nudged her a few times before licking a few smudges of blood from her face and neck. As if satisfied she was alive, he stepped back a few feet, his large, intelligent eyes meeting mine. I couldn't exactly read what was there, but I knew he wouldn't hurt us, that all he wanted was her safe.

I had no idea why he was so obsessed with this girl's safety, but I was grateful that he was. She had a way of making you want to watch out for her, so I guess I understood, at least on some level.

I nodded at him, silently thanking him for keeping her alive again, and then stood. Declan walked over to me, her hand ghosting across Max's face, as if she could wipe away the pain and anguish still visible in sleep.

"She's okay?" she asked, her words an echo of the grief I felt.

"Alive, at least," I said. It was enough. It had to be enough.

As one, we looked over at Atlas as he curled up against the spot Wade's body was pulled from, moments before. His wolfskin was shaking in uncontrollable sobs of pain, of rage. I couldn't bring myself to say anything about Wade—it was as if saying the word out loud would make it real somehow.

"We need to get her back, now." I looked down at her face, at her body covered in bloodied rags, and pressed her closer to my chest. It was like my brain was unconvinced she was alive, no matter how heavy she was in my arms or how soft her breaths were as they brushed against my skin.

Neither of us wanted to leave Atlas here, but one of us would have to. He couldn't come back with us, not like this. We couldn't handle another tragedy here tonight.

Rowan walked up and studied Max, his eyes filled with relief and reverence. He pulled her gently from my arms into his own, and I had to push back my instinct to resist him. If anyone could be trusted with her safety, I had to believe it was her brother.

"I'll stay with Atlas," Declan said, watching as Max was transferred to Rowan, her breathing an unusual rhythm, like she was crying in her sleep. "You should take them back. Call Seamus and Cyrus on your way and see where they are. They need to be filled in—on everything. Everything except—"

Except for the fact that Atlas was a wolf.

With a glance back at him, I met Declan's devastating eyes. I saw my grief mirrored there, the pain so acute that I had to look away. Without another word, Rowan and I started the impossibly long walk back to The Guild, our silence an echo of all that happened tonight, both of us filled with the abject fear of where we went from here.

DREAMS OF HELL

Grab Book Three in The Protector Guild series:

Max finally has everything she's always wanted: she's part of a team with her brother and best friend, she's spending her free time on missions hunting down evil monsters, and she's about to turn nineteen, the age protectors fully come into their power. Hell, she even gets to hang out with her favorite hellhound, Ralph, on her downtime. But it all still just feels empty, pointless even. Guilt is a bitch.

After last month's disaster, the members of Team Six abandoned Guild Headquarters, leaving Max alone to deal with the crippling shame for her part in the events that night. And she can't even blame them. If she could, she'd run away from all of this pain too. Attacks on campus mixed with dreams that leave her feeling more exhausted than refreshed, have her yearning for her simple life back home in the cabin and wishing that she never joined The Guild at all.

Losing focus when she's supposed to be hunting down all the

things that go bump in the night doesn't instill much confidence in her friends either. If she wants to secure an official spot on a team, she needs to snap out of her grief and become the protector she's always dreamed of becoming. And she needs to do it quickly. Attacks are happening in record numbers and the fate of her world is quite literally on The Guild's shoulders.

Just when she's starting to put the pieces of her life back together, Atlas and his team come barreling back into town to stir everything up again. Six is just as alluring as ever, only now she knows their big secret. The question is, does she follow her gut and protect them, or does she do what she's been trained to do and never look back?

Her family and The Guild may have trained her well when it comes to decapitating monsters, but they didn't train her for the one thing more difficult in this line of work...figuring out exactly who she can trust.

ACKNOWLEDGMENTS

This book wouldn't be possible without the support of my family and friends. You know who you are, and I couldn't be more grateful to have you in my life. Thanks for always encouraging me and pushing me to chase after my writing dreams.

Special thank you to my beta readers, my editor, Kath, and my cover designer, Michelle. This book is so much better because you've all contributed a piece to it. Thank you.

And to my very own 'Ralph,' thanks for keeping me company while I wrote this series for hours and months on end.

Printed in Great Britain
by Amazon